CYBER'S ESCAPE

Sapiens Run Book 2

JAMIE DAVIS

MedicCast Productions

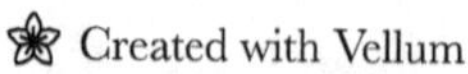 Created with Vellum

Sapiens Run Trilogy

Book 1 - *Cyber's Change*

Book 2 - *Cyber's Escape*

Book 3 - *Cyber's Underground*

—

The Delivery Mage (5 books)

Book 1 - *Deliver or Die*

—

The Broken Throne Series (5 books)

Read book 1 - *The Charm Runner*

—

The Accidental Traveler LitRPG Trilogy

(with C.J. Davis)

Read book 1 - *The Accidental Thief*

—

Accidental Champion Trilogy

(with C.J. Davis)

Read book 1 - *Accidental Duelist*

—

Extreme Medical Services Series (8 books)

Read book 1 - Extreme Medical Services

—

Eldara Sister Series (2 books)

Read book 1 - *The Nightingale's Angel*

—

Follow on Facebook for updates, news, and upcoming book excerpts

Facebook.com/jamiedavisbooks

—

To Madison and Hannah, the newest daughters in our growing family. It's exciting to see the example you both set taking on the world that awaits you. Take no prisoners, ladies!

Chapter 1

CASS ARMSTRONG PECKED out the remaining characters of her answer to the essay question. With a tap of the send button, she completed the last of her first semester finals. Cass waited for the screen to clear, showing the university's testing system had received the exam. As a green check mark displayed, she stood and started towards the door.

She looked around the room as she left. It pleased her to see she wasn't the last person to finish the final exam. Cass had struggled initially in her classes, primarily because her ability to study for the exams was reliant upon using outdated technology. Her family's technophobia and fear of artificial intelligence systems had kept her from bringing the latest hardware to school.

That all changed after Cass had a jet ski accident during her fall break. The cybernetic implants she had received to fix her injured brain, right eye, and ear also enabled her to access the central AI network known as the Mantle. The add-on enhancements helped her to study more efficiently, record video and audio from all of her classes, and index them via a transcription app she'd downloaded.

The implant in Cass's head had likely made the difference between passing and failing this semester. She shook her head at the irony of it all. Cass still remembered when she had first awakened after her emergency surgery. She had been sure it meant the end of her life as she knew it.

Now Cass accessed the Mantle without a second thought and checked the network for messages as she headed for the elevators. Her inbox in the cloud received the query and returned the same response she'd received prior to the beginning of the exam two hours before.

Empty.

Cass had hoped for a message from her girlfriend, Shelby Moore. Shelby had gone home to Boston to be with her family after her brother was murdered. Cass missed her so much, her heart ached at times. She understood Shelby's need to be with family right now, but that didn't mean she had to like it.

As Cass stepped off the elevator on the ground floor of the Business School building, a familiar voice called out to her.

"Hey, Cassie," Lisa said from across the lobby.

"Oh, hi, Lisa. How are you?"

"Finally done my finals," Lisa replied. "I can't believe I had to wait and stay here until the very last day of exam week for my last test."

"Me, too. This was the exam I was most worried about, though. I'm glad I had the extra time to study."

"Hey, have you heard from Shelby at all?"

Cass nodded. "A few times. At first, she couldn't talk much. She was busy doing a lot of things with her family for the funeral over the last few weeks. Since then, I've heard from her every couple of days."

"She left so suddenly. Do you know if she's planning on coming back to school?"

"I hope so. I miss her, and I don't want her to throw away her hard work from this semester."

Lisa smiled. "You two made a great couple. I hope she comes back, too. I miss her laugh."

Cass smiled. She missed Shelby's laugh, too. It made her sad to think about how long it had been since she'd heard it. Cass decided to change the subject before things became too morose. "When are you leaving to go home?"

"My parents come to get me this afternoon. And you?"

"Mine are coming tomorrow. I'm kind of nervous, though."

"Yeah, aren't your folks kind of strict about things like…" Lisa reached up and tapped her own cerebral implant with her forefinger.

A grim smile crossed Cass's face. "Yeah, you could say that. I'm hoping I can keep them from finding out about it, though. That's why I have to head back to the dorm. I have a lot to do to get ready before my mom and dad get here in the morning."

Lisa waved goodbye. "Well, good luck. I'll see you next semester."

"Yeah, see you then."

Lisa turned off towards the student center as she left the building's entrance. Cass turned in the opposite direction and headed towards the edge of campus and the freshman dorms. She had some important errands to run this afternoon after she stopped by her room.

Cass's plan to hide the implant on the right side of her head and face began with a sort of disguise. She'd already gotten an artificial skin covering to hide the metal surface that extended from her right temple back over her ear. Her hair had finally grown back post-surgery, too, so it helped to conceal the implant on that side when she wore it down. The synthetic skin patch was the first line of defense and essential for keeping her parents from learning about her cybernetic parts.

That wasn't the only challenge Cass faced going home. The Sapiens Movement enclave in which her family lived was surrounded by a powerful and sensitive virtual firewall. It was that barrier that had her most concerned and it was the reason for the next part of her plan. It required a risky trip to a sketchy neighborhood downtown, alone. Because of that, Cass had been putting it off all week.

She checked the time in her system and picked up her pace. She was excited to get back to the dorm because she'd planned to chat with Shelby for the first time in two days when she got back after the test.

Cass hoped Shelby had worked out a way to finish her fall semester classes remotely from home. She'd still been working on getting the details squared away when she and Cass last chatted.

The eerily silent dorm was almost empty. Most of the students had completed their finals earlier in the week and had already headed home. The only person she saw was the upper-class dorm monitor, Mitch. He sat at the front desk in the lobby as Cass entered the building.

"Hi, Cassie. Remember you need to check out of your dorm room before you leave. There's a whole checklist we need to go over. Tomorrow's the last day."

"I know. I'm working on finishing up getting packed now. Everything else is going to stay here during the break until I return."

"Will Shelby be coming back, too?"

"That's what I hope. I think she'll have everything squared away at home by then. I have to go. She's supposed to drop in for a face chat soon."

Mitch nodded and went back to something he'd been doing on the desktop screen. Cass headed down the hallway towards her room. Her implant signaled the cybernetic lock on the dorm room door of her arrival. She heard the click of the deadbolt unlocking the door as she reached for the handle. Cass entered her room, dropping her purse on the desk before flopping down on the bed.

She lay there for a long time, staring at the ceiling, trying to decide what she would say to Shelby when they spoke. Things had been more than a little awkward between them since Shelby's sudden departure a few weeks before.

In the beginning, Cass viewed Shelby's return home as a betrayal. Shelby had lost her brother in a horrific series of events at the Sapiens Movement rally held not far from campus near City Hall. Cass knew the loss of her brother devastated her girlfriend. Cass hadn't come through it unscathed, either. In the struggle to get away from their vantage point on a nearby rooftop, Cass accidentally had shoved a man trying to stop them. He'd lost his balance near the roof's edge and fallen to the sidewalk.

Cass could still see the man's crumpled form lying on the sidewalk five stories below. The pool of blood spread out around his head on the pavement in a horrific splash of crimson. She shuddered at the thought of all she'd seen and done that day. The memory of the rally, recorded via her cybernetic eye and implant, kept her awake at night sometimes.

The man's death had been ruled an accident by the authorities. Cass had been able to find out that much with a cursory search of the Mantle news services the next day. That didn't mean the guilt over her part in his death didn't gnaw at her.

It didn't help that conspiracy theories had popped up immediately about the other things she'd seen on the rally's stage. Naysayers downplayed the veracity of the video. Those people said the deaths of the subs on the rally's stage were faked by those trying to discredit the Sapiens Movement.

Cass and Shelby both knew the viral video Cass had recorded wasn't fake at all. She'd seen up close and personal the moment Shelby's brother Eric was killed by the Sapiens First terrorist leader on stage in front of the cheering crowd.

Elena, Cass's sister, told her everyone back home in the Sapiens enclave had a multitude of potential theories about the video. A few of those theories included the belief that the video was somehow related to the mysterious death of a rally attendee who fell from a nearby rooftop.

The viral video of the events was now known as the Saturday Massacre. Shelby had grabbed the video wirelessly from Cass's implant and streamed it anonymously out to the entire nation. In the weeks since, it had become one of the most viewed videos of the year.

As if on cue, Cass's implant system chimed with an alert. She opened the automated message from her inbox. A newsfeed story popped up. The alerts she'd set up about anything regarding the video notified her when a news item on the subject posted.

She activated the link and the newsfeed began playing the video newscast in her mind. It featured an interview with the leader of the Sapiens Movement, Sterling Noble.

"Mr. Noble," the female news anchor asked, "how do you respond to the assertion that your movement was behind the deaths of the seven cyber human individuals two weeks ago?"

Sterling Noble offered the woman a sad smile. "How would you like me to respond? I have denied it in every way I can. The members of the Sapiens Movement are peaceful. Our aspirations are only political. The alleged events depicted in that video are still under investigation by our own internal security team. We believe the video is fake and are hard at work to find the source so that we can verify it was indeed fabricated."

"How can you say the video was fabricated when the bodies of the seven individuals who died were later found in an alley not too far from the location of the Sapiens rally downtown?"

"It is our belief that those unfortunate individuals were killed as part of the plot to undermine our important work. We are not what our opponents say we are. The other members of the Sapiens Movement and I are merely people who wish to live in peace, alone and away from all artificial intelligence and robotics. The implication that we were involved in any way with their deaths is laughable."

The leader of the Sapiens Movement moved forward in his seat, leaning towards the interviewer as he continued. "It is far more likely those people who died were involved in some criminal element among the cyber human community. It is well known to us how their subversive efforts have impacted the level of crime in the center of major metropolitan areas. They frequently use their enhanced cybernetics to take advantage of normal humans like myself and my followers. The video is further proof of their depravity."

"So, your assertion is that the video was a pretense to discredit the Sapiens Movement?"

"That's what I'm saying." Sterling Noble kept his gaze level and stared the news anchor down as if daring her to ask him another question.

The female reporter shifted in her chair. "Very well, then. We'll have to leave it there as I'm out of time for this segment. Mr. Noble, thank you for coming on the show. If you have information that you think would shed more light on this topic, you are welcome to return and share it with our audience at a later date."

"I will certainly do that, Nancy."

Cass shut down the video feed.

She found herself clenching her fists in anger. She'd heard it all before in other interviews, but to see the leader of the movement, a man she'd once respected, repeating the lies, only served to alienate Cass from her family even more.

How could they say Eric's death and the death of the others had been made up? She'd seen it with her own two eyes. Sterling Noble was a friend of her family and she'd grown up believing in everything he said. Now she felt betrayed by everything he and her parents stood for.

All these thoughts warred within Cass as she went over her plans to prepare for her trip back to the enclave.

Chapter 2

THE CHIME SOUNDED on the tablet sitting on Cass's desk. It shook her from the dark thoughts swirling inside her head. Sitting up on her bed, Cass checked her connection to the network to see who was calling. She jumped up and ran over to her desk when she saw it was Shelby.

Cass sat down in the chair and tapped the screen on her tablet to connect the video chat.

Shelby's beautiful face filled the screen, her dark hair hanging down in loose curls on either side.

"Hey, Shel. It's so good to see your face. How are you?"

Shelby smiled and nodded. "I'm doing better, Cass. Things have settled down a lot since the funeral."

"How did things go getting your classes squared away? Will the professors allow you to finish the rest of your assignments and testing remotely?"

"Yeah, they're going to let me take my final exams at a college close to our house that can proctor them for me. It looks like I'll be able to finish things up. It'll be a few weeks late, but the semester will get done nonetheless."

"That's great news. So, you do plan on coming back next semester, then?"

Shelby smiled. "That's the plan. I'm hoping we can see each other before then, though. Do you think you could get away from your parents to come up to Boston and see me?"

Cass hesitated. Once her parents learned about Shelby and her cybernetic enhancements, they'd barely talked to her. The thought of their daughter dating someone they considered subhuman was something that angered Cass's mom and dad to the point that they refused to bring it up on the few calls they'd had with their daughter.

"I don't know, Shelby. It might be hard for me to get away from the enclave once I go home."

A look of concern crossed Shelby's face and her brow furrowed. "You will be coming back to school next semester, too, won't you?"

Cass shrugged. "I assume so. I haven't heard anything different from them, though, to be honest, we've hardly talked since you left. Still, they've invested in me to come here. The money would be wasted if they didn't let me finish my degree."

"You don't sound so sure of yourself."

Cass shook her head. "It's not that. Coming back to school's the least of my worries. I'm more concerned about them finding out about my own implants. If they discover what happened to me and how the doctor's fixed me, I don't know what they'll do."

"You've got your skin patch to cover up the cerebral implant. Everything else is internal. As long as you keep that hidden, you should be able to keep them from learning about everything, right?"

Cass gave half a smile. "That's the plan, at least part of it, anyway."

"What else is there, Cass? Is there something you're not telling me?"

"There's one more problem that most people outside the enclaves don't know about. We keep it a secret to make sure we can catch people who might try to infiltrate our communities."

Shelby's puzzled frown prompted Cass to keep going. She had to tell Shelby eventually. "Shel, the enclave perimeter has security systems and an impenetrable firewall that sounds an alarm when any Mantle-connected device or person crosses the boundaries of the community enclosure. I'm afraid that's going to be my downfall. I've tried searching the Mantle for alternatives in my spare time, but I've been unable to discover anything that can help me."

"You should go back to the Bizarre, Cass. I'd be willing to bet someone there can get a workaround figured out for you."

Cass nodded. "That was my initial thought, too. I plan on going down there tonight. The problem is, I wouldn't even know who to talk to. Do you know of someone there who might be able to help me?"

"Remember the guy who created your skin patch, Frederick? He might be able to help you. He's mastered the physical way to cover up an implant. You can't be the first person who's needed to hide it from detection systems, too."

"That's not a bad idea," Cass said. "My parents come to get me tomorrow morning, sometime after ten o'clock. I don't have much time."

"You should get down to the Bizarre sooner rather than later then."

Shelby looked off into space for a second. Cass realized she was checking something online via her implant.

"It's already 4 p.m. They may already be closing up by the time you get there. I don't know how many of the vendors will stay late on a Friday like this. You have to hurry, Cass."

Cass didn't want to end her conversation with Shelby. They talked so infrequently now. "All right, I'll go. Promise I can call you later?"

Shelby shrugged. "I'll see. My parents wanted to do something just the three of us this evening. There've been family and friends over nearly every day since the funeral. Today's the first day we've had to ourselves. Mom thought it might help us adjust to the new family dynamic without Eric if we did something together tonight."

Cass smiled to be supportive, even though she didn't feel it inside. The challenges Shelby's family faced were ones she couldn't even fathom. She certainly didn't want to get in the way of their family healing from the violent loss of a son and brother. This might be the last chance to talk to Shelby for a while, though.

Cass knew she'd be unable to talk with her girlfriend much at all once she got home with her parents. The enclave's security firewall worked both ways. They blocked unwanted things coming and going.

Cass smiled in spite of her disappointment. "Well, try and call me later when your family is finished with whatever outing your parents have planned. I'll make sure I'm awake whenever you call."

"I'll try. Bye, Cass. Good luck at the Bizarre."

"Bye, Shel," Cass replied. "I love you."

"I love you, too."

The screen went blank. In Cass's mind, the blankness extended inside her as well. She wondered if Shelby would call her later or not. Managing their relationship at a distance like this was more difficult than she'd imagined it would be.

Cass had wanted to hold Shelby close to her and go back to the way it was before for two weeks now. She couldn't endure being away from her for nearly two more months while on their winter break.

She pushed the gloomy thoughts away and reminded herself she needed to get downtown to the Bizarre, the underground marketplace for cybernetic enhancements. It was a fantastic resource and Cass had already considered going there for help with her problem.

Shelby was right, though. It was getting late on a Friday afternoon. Some of the vendors would start packing up to go home before too long.

Cass grabbed her purse from the desk and left to head downtown. It was time to find a way past the Sapiens restrictive cybernetics firewall.

The driverless auto cab dropped Cass at the curb across the street from the alley leading to the Bizarre's entrance. She checked traffic and then crossed the road, heading down into the alley between two apartment buildings. She reached the steel door on the right leading to the marketplace and pulled it open. The metal stairwell echoed as she descended to the abandoned underground parking garage.

Cass chuckled when she reached the bottom and stepped out into the open space filled with tables and stalls. It was funny to think of coming here by herself. The first time she'd come here, she'd been frightened of everything about this place. She was new to her cybernetic enhancement and didn't trust people in the cyber human community the way she did now. She'd had to fight past all of the prejudices she'd grown up with. Along the way, she'd learned there were people just like her who wanted to live their lives, enhancements and all.

Cass crossed the garage, walking down the rows of tables hoping the vendor known as The Skin Doctor was down there in his usual spot. Shelby had been right about the vendors packing up for the night. A bunch of the stalls were starting to tear down early. She saw more than a few vendors packing up their wares in bins and totes and rolling them towards the freight elevator at the far end of the garage.

Cass hurried down the last aisle towards the far corner. That was where Frederick, also known as The Skin Doctor, had set up his booth when she was here the last time. A wave of relief washed over her when she saw him standing there talking to a woman with a cybernetic arm similar to Shelby's.

Frederick smiled at Cass as she approached. "If you give me just a few minutes, my dear, I'll be with you as soon as I can."

"No problem," Cass replied. "I can wait."

The woman talking to the former plastic surgeon smiled at Cass and continued her discussion. "So, you can come up with a reliable covering or glove that will hide my arm?"

"I can. There are some challenges though."

"Like what?"

"The larger the surface area I need to cover, the harder it is to get the skin tension right. The elasticity of normal skin is different than what I use in my materials. Over time, a larger covering will start to sag in certain stressed areas like the wrist and elbow. The smaller the sleeve is, the easier it is for me to create and repair if necessary."

"I need this job, Doc. I need to make money to feed my children. They won't hire me if they know I have a cybernetic arm."

"If you wear something with long sleeves, I should be able to make something that goes up your forearm almost to your elbow. That will cover up everything in view as long as you keep your sleeve down. When do you need it?"

"As soon as possible. I have an interview on Monday."

Frederick looked up at the ceiling and tapped his chin. "Hmmm, I can probably make that work. I won't have it for you until Monday morning, though. I need to use the larger 3-D printer I have at my house. Meet me here first thing. I already have the measurements on your arm. There might be a few last-minute adjustments that need to be made, but I can handle that before your interview."

"Thank you, Doc. You don't know what this means to me."

"I do, which is why I am making an effort to get it done faster than I normally would be able to. Things have gotten more difficult for us in recent weeks. It seems as if the supporters of Sterling Noble and his cronies have become more open in their persecution of us in spite of what happened here in the city a few weeks ago."

The woman nodded with understanding. "I would have thought they'd back down and keep a low profile after the horrible things his followers did. Let's hope things settle down soon. Anyway, I'll be back on Monday. Have a good weekend and thank you."

The Skin Doctor smiled and nodded at the woman then turned to Cass. "It's Cassie, isn't it?"

"Yes," Cass replied, as she reached out to shake the former doctor's hand. "You helped me with a skin patch for my cheek to hide my implant."

"Is there a problem?" He reached up to tilt Cass's head to one side and studied the side of her face, searching for signs of any issues.

"Oh, no, everything's fine with that. It's excellent work, really. It's just that I am getting ready to go home for this semester and will be living there for almost two months over winter break. I'm afraid that my family might detect something."

Frederick snapped his fingers. "Oh, that's right. I'd forgotten your family were Sapiens Movement members. You have to go home and live inside one of the enclaves, right?"

Cass nodded, a grim look across her face.

Frederick frowned. "That poses a problem, doesn't it, because you need a way around the security protocols."

Hope filled Cass. He understood her situation, so he must have a solution. "You act like you've done this before. Do you have a way around the enclave security firewall?"

He smiled. "You're not the first person who's had to go into one of the enclaves while hiding who they were. There are always alternatives. I can't do it, though. That type of hack is far beyond my meager programming skills. I'll have to put you in touch with somebody with the ability to install a custom firmware update for your implant. Are you okay with that?"

The blood drained from Cass's face as she blanched at the idea of someone tinkering with the cybernetic programming interfacing with her brain. That particular option hadn't occurred to her.

"Is that really necessary?"

"I'm afraid it is. You need new firmware installed to enable your implant to cover its AI signature and electronic serial number so it looks like any other dumb computer interface, like a typical tablet. The enclave will just think it's a standard piece of electronics and let you pass without a problem."

"Will that in any way diminish the implant's functionality? Mine isn't just for cosmetic purposes. I had an injury and it performs vital functions in my brain."

"Derek will be able to figure that out. That's one of the reasons I wouldn't even attempt working on it. Ordinarily, I'd just tell folks to shut down the cerebral interface entirely and go dark while crossing into a location like that. In your situation, you need a complete hack of the system. Derek's a good fellow and he does excellent work. Oh, and don't be afraid of his initial demeanor. He's a bit eccentric, but mostly harmless."

Cass wondered what that meant. She needed this upgrade to go home, but the whole thing sounded more than a little shady.

"I'll send you the details directly via my implant to yours. I also just sent him a message copying you on it so you two recognize each other when you get there."

"Are you sure he'll be home?"

Frederick laughed. "Definitely. He never goes outside. He doesn't trust anyone. That's a good thing, though. His paranoia is what makes him such a genius."

A signal pinged in Cass's head. A new message appeared with an address and a name, Derek Cross. She nodded. "Got it. Thank you, Doctor."

"Good luck going home, young lady. When you get back next semester, make sure you come by and let me know how things went."

"I will. Take care and enjoy the upcoming holidays."

He nodded and turned back to continue his work on something inside the small 3-D printer behind him. Cass crossed the garage back to the stairwell and left the Bizarre heading back up to the street.

She signaled for an auto cab via her connection to the Mantle. The address was all the way across town and Cass wanted to hurry. It was already getting late. The sun had set while she was down inside the marketplace.

Cass buried her apprehension at heading to one of the rougher sections of the city at this time of night. She had no choice. She had to get this installation over with before her parents arrived the next morning or everything would fall apart.

Chapter 3

WHEN SHE REACHED the address Frederick gave her, a little voice in the back of Cass's mind found it amusing she'd been so afraid of the inner-city neighborhood surrounding the building housing the Bizarre. Apparently, she had no idea what a genuinely rough neighborhood looked like.

Now she did.

Trash filled the gutters on either side of the street and all of the buildings on both sides were run down and in ill repair. Someone, or a group of someones, had broken out a lot of the windows at street level.

Based on the broken windows and the way the doors hung off some of the hinges in the building entrances, Cass assumed most of the buildings were abandoned in this area. That included the four-story row-home in front of which she now stood.

Cass took a deep breath. She couldn't afford to be squeamish or let her fear rule her. Cass hesitated before starting up the broad stone steps leading to the front door.

She dialed in her ocular implant to enable night vision capability. Everything took on a greenish tint. She could see much better now. Even the darkest corners of the hallway visible through the broken window in the upper half of the door stood out clearly to her enhanced vision.

Cass didn't have to worry about the door being locked, because there was neither lock nor door handle. Both had been broken off. It looked like someone had forced the door open at some point with a crowbar or some other tool. She gripped the splintered wood on the door's exposed edge and pulled it open with ease, stepping inside.

There were no lights visible in the interior. In fact, it didn't appear there was any working power in the building at all. That didn't matter to Cass, though. Her cybernetic eye easily compensated for the low light levels. She saw not only what was visible in the normal light spectrum, but also in the infrared and ultraviolet ranges as well. Navigating in the dark was no problem for her.

Cass looked around the first floor of the dilapidated row home. She didn't see anyone or any signs of habitation. Each of the rooms was strewn with trash and debris. It appeared that people might stay here from time to time, based upon the empty food containers amidst the garbage, but no one was present right now.

Cass stopped searching the first floor and started back towards the front of the building to climb the stairs to the second floor. She stopped when she heard a voice coming from behind her.

"Who's up there?" A man's voice called. He sounded far off in the distance. Based on the burst of static Cass heard along with it, whomever it was, spoke to her over a hidden speaker somewhere on the first floor. "I can hear you walking around. Who are you?"

Cass turned around. The voice came from the rear of the house. Cass headed down the hallway towards the area that was formerly the kitchen. All of the appliances had been ripped out. Even the sink and pipes had been removed. It had all probably been sold for scrap metal.

A door was ajar in the corner and she noticed a dim glow of light coming up out of it. The light had definitely not been there before when she poked her head in earlier during her initial search.

"Dammit, I asked who's up there?"

It came from the open doorway.

Cass moved to the door where she saw steps leading to the basement. She decided to answer the mysterious voice. Maybe this was Derek.

"It's me, Cass Armstrong. Frederick should have sent you a message about me coming to see you?"

"Yeah, I got the message. I'm not sure what you want from me, though. I don't like visitors."

Cass almost turned around and left. Only her fear of what her parents would do when her secret was discovered held her in place.

Summoning the courage to stand up for herself, she cleared her throat and said, "I need your help, Derek. I come from a Sapiens Movement enclave. My parents are coming to pick me up at school tomorrow and I can't let them find out about my implants. You have to see me. I have nowhere else to go."

Cass pulled open the basement door and stood at the top of the stairs waiting for an answer.

After standing there for what seemed like forever, the man on the speaker answered her. "Fine. You can come down. I make no promises but I'll hear you out. Pull the door shut behind you. I don't need anyone else poking around down here."

Cass stepped into the stairway, starting down the steps. She pulled the door shut behind her until it latched, then turned and continued downstairs. The dim glow of light came from beneath a door at the bottom of the steps.

Cass opened the door and entered a basement filled with multiple lifetimes of forgotten belongings, trash, and broken furniture. She scanned the room but found no sign of the strange man she was here to see.

"Derek? Where are you?"

"Cross the basement until you find another door. Your enhanced vision should be able to see a sliver of light under it."

Cass froze. How did he know about her cybernetic eye? This was more than a little creepy and for the second time she almost turned around and left.

If Frederick was right about this guy, he might just be paranoid enough to scan people coming into his nest, lair, or whatever he called this place. Fear held Cass back for a few seconds from going any further alone. She stood rooted to the spot while she gathered her courage.

Gritting her teeth, Cass walked across the basement, weaving around the old furniture stacked down there amidst the piles of refuse until she came to the door Derek described. Mounted next to the door was an old circular car stereo speaker. An ancient hand-held camcorder from a previous century was wired to a bracket above it. The camera's red light was lit.

"Open the door and come on down."

It took a couple of tugs to pull the old wooden door open. It was wedged tightly in the frame. When Cass finally managed to open it, she found another staircase leading downward. This one was concrete and there were small, but bright, LED lights spaced along the ceiling all the way down.

She smiled into the camera, realizing Derek had been watching her the whole time. There were probably hidden cameras upstairs she hadn't noticed. Maybe he was just as scared as she was.

Ratcheting up some additional courage and channeling a little of what she thought Shelby would do in a situation like this, Cass said, "Derek, if you want me to go down these stairs, you'd better tell me how much farther I have to go until I reach you. I'm a girl walking alone at night here. I'm not going to stumble into your lair so you can kidnap me or something?"

"Kidnap you? What kind of guy do you think I am?"

"The kind of guy who lives in creepy dark basements and secret tunnels." Cass stopped talking and waited for a response at the top of the steps.

Derek didn't answer for a long time. When he did, it wasn't over the intercom.

After a series of strange clicking sounds from below, a small, rotund figure walked to the bottom of the steps and stared up at her. The tiny man couldn't have been more than four feet tall. He walked on metal prosthetic enhancements instead of legs. The gray metal stilts ended in what looked like normal, bare human feet, though. The whole thing appeared very strange to Cass.

"Now that you can see me," Derek asked from the bottom of the stairway, "Are you still afraid?"

Cass smiled. She'd been right. He lived hidden down here because he was just as frightened as she was. "Thank you, Derek. I appreciate you coming out to see me."

Cass descended the stairs, reaching the bottom and following the little man down a long concrete corridor until they reached a steel door with at least a dozen locks and deadbolts scattered across the surface. Derek pulled the door open and gestured for her to enter.

Cass spotted a modest square room on the far side. There was a bed, a table with one chair, a small refrigerator, and cook stove with two coiled electric burners, all sitting opposite a desk that filled the wall to the right. The desk was covered in computer monitors and holographic displays. She saw a video feed scrolling through images of the rest of the building above.

After a brief hesitation, Cass stepped inside. Derek followed her, closing the door with a clang. As the door shut, all of the locks activated, each latching with a distinct click until all had sealed the door tightly. That explained the clicking sounds she'd heard from the top of the stairs.

"Hey, you're gonna let me out of here, right?"

Derek gestured around the room and smiled. "Of course. There's no room in here for two of us to live. It's just a security measure. Now, what do you want?"

Cass took a deep breath and started explaining her situation. "I need a way to get past the perimeter security wards of a Sapiens enclave. Is that something you can help me with?"

"Why would you want to go back into a place like that? You did it. You escaped. Make a run for it and be free while you still can. A girl like you would get chewed up and spit out by those animals. Didn't you see the video of what happened at the Saturday Massacre?"

Cass resisted the urge to scream at him that she knew all too well what happened at the Saturday Massacre, but she held her tongue. "I have my reasons. I just want to know if you can do it. So, what's the answer?"

"Oh, it can be done. It's not easy and some precautions have to be taken, but I can do it. Those protocols are constantly updated and changed. You could get a patch today and find out tomorrow that it won't work anymore. The big challenge is to create an interactive and flexible system that hides your identity from the sensors so that you can come and go safely without being detected and stay hidden while inside no matter what happens."

"And?" Cass asked.

"That's why you were sent here. Frederick told you he thought I could do it. He wasn't wrong. He just wasn't sure I would do it, that's all."

Derek squinted his eyes as he looked up at Cass. He appeared to be examining her face for something. "You still haven't told me why you want to go back into one of those places. A pretty thing like you should want to stay away from the lion's den."

"Why do you need to know that? It's none of your business."

"It is my business. If they discover I'm giving out this kind of technology and software, they're going to come down here for me. I need to know you're worth risking a Sapiens First hit squad for. I also need to know you're not going to turn me in, if they discover you're there."

Cass thought about what Derek said. A few months before she'd have called him crazy for believing in the mythical Sapiens First arm of the movement. Now she knew too well how real they were. She'd seen the horrible things they were willing to do to protect the movement's views.

Cass leaned forward, peering down at the small man standing in front of her. She had to convince him to help her. "Fine, Derek, you want to know why I need to get inside? It's because I was born there. My family lives there and I have to go back there now that the semester is finished."

"Your family doesn't know about your implants?"

Cass shook her head.

Derek cocked his head to the side as he looked up at her, examining her face. "You're putting yourself at risk, girlie."

Tears suddenly filled Cass's eyes. She was tired of explaining all of this, tired of being afraid. "I don't have anywhere else to go. If I don't return home, I'll lose everything. I won't be able to go back to school or anything else. I need to keep them from learning about what happened to me so I can go on with my life."

Derek continued studying her face. Then he nodded. "Hmmph, I'll do it. It's a bad idea to go back, but I'll help you if that's what you're determined to do."

He shook his head as he turned and waddled over to his desk. He climbed up onto the chair in front of it and sat down with his metal legs dangling over the front, the toes wiggling as if they were real feet. Cass smiled despite her situation at the peculiar image it presented. Derek began tapping away at a virtual keyboard which appeared in the air above the desk.

The machines and monitors on the desktop hummed to life. Lights began blinking across several different devices sitting here and there on top of the desk. Several of the monitors started scrolling lines of what appeared to be some sort of computer code.

Cass studied it all, unaware of what she was looking at. She realized she was taking a huge chance here, but she was right when she told Derek she had no choice. She could only hope this strange little man knew what he was talking about.

"How long will it take?" Cass asked.

"I need to compile a new set of instructions for the software. It changes every time they update their systems in the enclaves. That reminds me, which enclave are you from? They're all a little different."

"The Pottstown one, outside of Philly. How will you know what makes that one different?"

"People like me have set up sensors outside all the Sapiens enclaves for years to monitor their security protocols. The guy who runs the Pottstown enclave is particularly devious and paranoid. This is going to be tricky."

"You can do it, though, right?"

"He's good. Top notch really when you consider where he lives and works. He's not better than me, though." Derek hooked a thumb over his shoulder without turning away from his screens.

"You might want to sit down and relax. It's going to be a while. Probably a few hours or more."

Cass looked around. The only other chair in the room was the one next to the small table beside the stove unit and refrigerator. It had a stack of dirty clothes on it. She carefully moved the clothing to the cot in the corner and sat down on the chair.

She didn't have anything else to do so she began searching for some music to stream in over her connection to the Mantle. That was when she first realized she was completely cut off from any wireless signals. How had she not noticed that when she came down here?

"Hey, I can't connect. What's up?"

"Of course, you can't connect. Nobody can connect from down here. That's how I hide."

Cass became slightly annoyed. Derek didn't even bother to turn around when he answered her. He just kept tapping away on the virtual keyboard while he worked on whatever it was he was doing. "How come you can connect on your computers then?"

"That's why I live in this house, girlie. It's built right over an old T-4 fiber-optic data line. I'm jacked directly into the connection to the Mantle with a hardwired line. Everybody's so busy looking for wireless signals these days, nobody even thinks about trying to track down connections to the network over the old fiber cables."

Cass didn't even know what a T-4 line was. She shrugged and sat back, occupying herself by reading the book she'd downloaded to her implant a week before.

Hours later, just before she reached the climax in the book, the tiny man slapped his hand down on top of the desk and said, "Got it."

"What?" Cass asked.

"I finally got it to work. For some reason, when I updated with the new changes in the security system at the Pottstown enclave, it caused my software to crash, repeatedly. That kind of pissed me off because I had to start over and write new code from scratch. It would've been nasty if that happened while it was installed in your implant. It would have caused your implant to fry itself. Whoever's running things over there has got a really nasty sense of humor. He's not just trying to stop people from entering with implants, he's intent on injuring or killing them just for going through the gates."

"Wait, what? I don't want my implant fried. It'll kill me."

Derek waved his hand in the air. "Don't worry about it. I've got it figured out. Weren't you listening to what I said?"

He hopped off his seat and reached into a bin under his desk. He pulled out a shiny metal tube that looked suspiciously like the one police used to disable implants for prisoners taken into custody. Cass had first-hand experience with one of those. It wasn't pleasant.

"Hey, I don't want you using that thing on me."

"Relax, it's not the same as the ones police use or the one that Sapiens First goon used to kill the cybers in the Saturday Massacre video. I've modified it quite significantly. Its built-in wireless control interface is still the best way to connect and control large sections of the systems in a cerebral implant. Let me just load my custom software on here and then we'll give it a try and see if we can get it to download."

Cass didn't like the idea of trying to download new software into her cerebral implant. It frightened her more than a little.

Derek finished doing whatever it was he had to do with the electronic tube. He slid off his chair and came across the floor to stand next to Cass where she sat in his rickety wooden chair.

"Hold still. If you move, it could screw everything up. This might be a little uncomfortable."

Cass sat up straight, holding herself rigid while she stared out of the corner of her eye at the metal tube approaching the right side of her face. Derek waved the end of the tube about a quarter of an inch away from the implant.

A faint hum rose in the background as he thumbed a switch on the end of the device. A tingling sensation tickled the sensors inside her head. It was curious because it wasn't a physical sensation at all. It was more like the memory of such a feeling. There was a flash of warmth and then a brief stab of pain that caused Cass to gasp.

"Hold still, girl," Derek hissed. "We're only halfway there."

"What are you doing to me? I'm feeling all sorts of strange things going on."

"The software has to mesh with all of the systems controlled by your implant. You have quite an extensive upgrade there. There's a lot of stuff going on in there according to what I can see over my read out. You're probably feeling the different systems that control sensations around your body being integrated in with my software. Everything has to work together or it won't do what it needs to do."

Cass closed her mouth, gritting her teeth against the now persistent and uncomfortable ache in the right side of her head. At one point she wanted to scream. It felt like a million tiny ants were crawling under the skin on both arms. Just when she couldn't bear it any longer, it stopped.

Derek lowered the tube and flipped the switch. The faint hum faded away.

"That should do it, girlie. Why don't you go in and search your implant's system for a file called *protocol one*?"

Cass found the file Derek pointed her towards. It popped up immediately upon searching the database and memory inside her implant. "I found it. Now what?"

"That is the installation file for when you arrive back at the enclave. It's important that you run that program while you're still outside the gates, but close enough for your implant to detect the security firewall."

Cass shook her head. She didn't know how to do this kind of thing. "How close is that? I'm not sure I will have an excuse to wait outside the gate while some program runs in my head."

"You have to wait. The diagnostics system in the program has to operate to update your systems to any firewall upgrades that might have been added between now and then. Once it runs and notifies you it's complete, you can slide past the firewall without a care in the world. If you don't follow the instructions, the system will alert to your presence immediately upon passing through the gates."

Part of Cass thought that would be what happened no matter what she did. She only partially believed this system was even going to work. "How do I know you've done what you said?"

"You won't until you pass through the gates for the first time. I'm sorry, but there's no way to know for sure. Plus, you have to run the update every day when you wake up and maybe again at night, too. They upgrade the systems there frequently. You'll have to reset the *protocol one* patch each day while you're inside to avoid detection."

Cass got up, nodded, and pointed to the door. This was all overwhelming her. "Let me out. I need some air."

Derek pulled a tiny remote with a single button on it from his pocket. He pointed it at the door and pressed the button. The locks all clicked open at the same time.

"You've never been a prisoner here, Cass. All you had to do was ask if you wanted to leave. I know you might doubt that my program will help you. It will, though. You only have to run the system and give it enough time to do its job."

"How long will that take?"

Derek shrugged. "It's hard to say. My guess is probably a minute or two. It all depends on what new upgrades have been added to the firewall between now and then. Part of the program will download updated patches from my local system here. The size and number of patches will determine the time needed to upgrade your implant. I'm sorry, but that's the best answer I can give you."

Cass shrugged. Her exhaustion at being up half the night was catching up with her. "I guess it'll have to be good enough. Goodbye Derek. Thank you."

"Good luck to you, girlie. If you ever get back this way, let me know how it all worked out."

Cass nodded and proceeded out the door. Soon she was back up the steps to the main floor. It was after midnight and she had a lot of packing to do before her parents arrived later that morning.

Chapter 4

CASS WOKE up the next morning. She'd only slept for a few hours, having spent most of the night packing. She rubbed her eyes as she headed to the cafeteria for her final breakfast at school that semester. She was so tired and needed coffee to help her wake up before her parents arrived.

As she sat alone eating, Cass realized how much she missed spending meal time with Shelby. In the two weeks since she'd been gone, Cass had had to do a lot of adjusting to not having her girl-friend around all of the time.

The time apart also forced Cass to do a lot of the things needed to maintain her implant and its omnipresent access to the Mantle and the connected devices all around her. She'd only had the implant for a few months and Cass was still settling into using the device in her head along with all of the capabilities it brought with it.

One of the things she recently discovered was that she could track anyone with a cell phone signal on the network. It had surprised her to see their location on a map when she reached out to check for any messages from her father or mother. Her implant popped up a link to a map showing their location at home inside the enclave.

Cass wondered if her father even knew this was available to the system. He'd probably never carry a cell phone again if he was aware that anyone connected to the Mantle could track his every move.

Because of that feature in her implant, Cass had been able to set up alerts notifying her when her parents left the enclave that morning. The signal pinged her while she carried her breakfast dishes back up to the window to drop them off after finishing her meal.

The message from her implant gave an ETA telling her she had about two hours to finish getting packed up and ready to go. She'd done most of her packing the night before but still had a lot to do to before going home with her parents.

Cass hustled back to her room and started throwing the last of her clothes into the suitcase open on her bed. She got an empty cardboard box from the recycling dumpster behind the dorm to use for the last pile of things from her desk.

She'd just finished packing the last of the items when the alert in her head chimed once more, notifying Cass of her parents' arrival at the front doors of the dorm. She kept an eye on the dorm's hallway cameras as she watched her parents come down the hallway towards her room.

Cass glanced in the mirror one last time as her fingers traced the slight ridge above her cheek running back to her right ear. Her fingertips couldn't detect any seam between her real skin and the artificial skin patch over her implant. She nodded as she straightened her hair to make sure it covered most of the area. It served as a backup in case the skin patch worked loose somehow. With her hair grown back, she no longer needed the wig she'd purchased. She left that in the dresser drawer. As her parents arrived at the door to her dorm room, Cass took a deep breath and opened it before they had a chance to knock.

"Hi, Mom. Hi Dad. I'm all set to go home."

Cass wasn't sure how her parents were going to react to seeing her. This was the first time they'd seen each other in person since her father's discovery of Shelby's cyber human status.

Her dad's awkward smile at his daughter didn't seem genuine to her. She thought it appeared a little forced. He entered the room and pointed at the collection of boxes and the suitcase on the bed. "Is this everything you're bringing home with you?"

"Ummm, yeah. I think I've got everything I need."

Cass's dad grunted as he picked up one of the boxes. "All right then, I'll start carrying things out to the car." He headed through the door and down the hallway.

There was a moment of awkward silence as Cass and her mother stood alone in the room. They'd only said a few words to each other over face chat calls in the past few weeks. Cass wanted to go over and hug her. She needed reassurance her mom still loved her. Cass missed both her parents desperately, especially since Shelby had gone home.

It was her mom who initiated the conversation, breaking the silence as she walked over to Cass's desk. "Are you sure you have everything you need? We aren't going to be able to turn around and come back if you've forgotten anything. Your father and I have a dinner to go to tonight after we get home."

"I have everything. I'm sure."

Her mom pointed to the dresser and crossed over to it. She pulled open the top drawer. "You've double checked everything, right?" She glanced inside and reached in, pulling out Cass's wig.

Cass froze, assuming her mother would see through the deception immediately. She struggled as her mind whirled through possible explanations, trying to come up with a reason for having the wig in her dresser.

"What's this?"

"Oh, that's a wig, Mom. You've seen wigs before."

"Very funny. I know it's a wig. Why do you have a wig that looks just like your hair?"

"Ummm, it's from a costume party. I went dressed as Shelby and she went dressed as me."

Her mother stiffened as soon as Cass mentioned Shelby's name.

She dropped the wig as if it were suddenly on fire and slid the drawer closed. "We'll leave that here, then."

Cass didn't wait for any further comments from her mother on the subject. It would only cause a fight. Instead, she said, "We should help Dad carry the stuff out. It's going to take us all several trips."

"Good idea. Let's get this over with so we can head home."

Cass picked up a box from her bed. Her mother did the same. The two of them headed out to the car as Cass sighed. She'd managed to dodge a lot of awkward questions from her mother regarding the wig she'd used to hide her implant while her hair grew back.

A half-hour later, Cass turned in her key card to Mitch at the dorm's front desk in the lobby. He had her sign out on a tablet with a checklist stating that she'd completed locking down her room during winter break.

"I look forward to seeing you back in about a month and a half, Cass."

"Yeah, me too," Cass said. "Enjoy your break, Mitch."

"You, too."

Cass turned and headed outside. Her parents waited in the car at the curb. She climbed into the back seat and her father pulled away onto the street, heading towards the interstate to take them north towards the enclave.

Cass's nervousness had her feeling jittery all over. It wasn't just the possibilities for an awkward conversation with her parents on the drive home. She was just as afraid of there being no conversation at all because they were still angry with her. And then there were her worries about getting through the enclave's security firewall.

She double checked her memory bank, verifying the *protocol one* file was still in place. There was a pop-up notice attached to the file when she looked at it. She opened the notification to find a text message from Derek.

Cass glanced up at her parents in the front seat. They sat talking quietly about something to do with the neighbors back home. She returned to concentrating on her implant's internal interface and played the short video message attached to the notification. Only she could hear it since it played inside her implant's direct cerebral interface.

"Cass, my system notified me that the administrator of the enclave security protocol uploaded a new version right after you left. I've included a link in this notification for you to download an updated version of the protocol one file. Make sure you do that before you arrive. Otherwise, it's likely the existing version will not allow you to pass through undetected."

Cass rechecked the notification. There was a clickable link at the end of the message. She activated it and approved the download of the new version of the file. Cass settled back and closed her eyes, resting as the file downloaded in the background. Maybe it would be all right if she didn't talk to her parents after all. She needed to be alone with her thoughts.

Having this new file downloading made her nervous and she was afraid she'd say something that would tip them off. Cass closed her eyes and drifted off to sleep. The system in her implant automatically updated the file while she slept.

Chapter 5

CASS JOLTED awake as something brushed against her arm. She looked around, getting her bearings as her mother said, "Wake up Cassie. We finally got you home."

Cass recognized the familiar painted tan stucco of the enclave's walls passing her window. With shock, she realized they were driving up to the black iron gates at the entrance to the Sapiens Movement compound she called home. She was supposed to start running the *protocol one* file before she got this close to the sensor systems.

Cass couldn't afford to let her father drive through those gates, not yet.

"Stop."

"What's wrong?" her father asked. He stopped the car just before turning into the entrance. The gate had already started opening. It had sensed the car's arrival and recognized the sensor installed in the car's license plate bracket as it approached.

She had to think quickly. Cass knew she only had a few seconds before her father continued on and passed through the gates. That would trigger the security alarms for sure. Cass didn't know if it was already too late or not.

"I want you to take a picture of me and Mom, Dad. I want to

celebrate my homecoming. Let's get out here by the community's sign. Come on, we took one by the sign at school at the beginning of the semester. This will commemorate my return home."

Not waiting for an answer, Cass removed her seat belt and opened her door to get out.

Cass's mom did the same. "Let's just take the picture so we can get home, James."

Her father didn't look convinced. Cass knew he hated doing this kind of thing, even when on family vacations and outings. She could tell what he really wanted was to get back to the house.

Cass jumped out onto the street, walking around the front of the car and across the broad strip of grass to stand by the enclave's sign notifying passersby they were entering the Sapiens community.

Noble Haven
  an AI restricted neighborhood.

"Come on, Mom. Let's get that picture." As soon as she said it, Cass activated the *protocol one* installation program inside her cerebral implant. Immediately, the diagnostics started querying nearby systems. A notification popped up telling her it found the enclave's firewall.

As she posed next to her mother, the program Derek had created and installed in Cass's head started assessing the new upgrades to the firewall. A status bar filled a screen in the corner of her mind. It was moving way too slow as it filled from left to right.

Cass's mom climbed out of the front passenger seat and walked over to stand next to Cass by the sign. She reached out and pulled her daughter close with an arm across her shoulders. She didn't say anything to Cass, though. Instead, she turned back to her husband. "James, honey. Get out and come over here so you can take the picture."

Cass thought she could actually hear her father grind his teeth over her enhanced auditory inputs, but it could have been her imagination. With an exasperated sigh, he climbed out, pulling his phone from his pocket.

He walked around to the front of the car so he could get both of them in the frame and held up his phone so the camera faced them. When he spoke, his tone told Cass how annoyed he was at this little diversion as he said, "Say cheese."

Cass and her mother both replied, "Cheese." Her mother didn't sound like she was all that into the photo op either.

Her dad tapped the screen of his phone once and then slid it back into his pocket. "There, I took the picture. Now, let's get in the car and go home."

She and her mother started back towards the car's passenger side while her dad climbed back into the front seat behind the wheel. Cass checked the status bar of the program loading in her implant. The diagnostics still ran, searching the firewall program for its security protocols. The status bar was only about half full. By her estimation, it would take at least another minute or two to complete its system check and make the necessary upgrades to her firmware.

"If it's all right with both of you, Mom and Dad, I think I'll walk back. I miss the old neighborhood and want to take a look around before I get home."

Both her parents glared at her from the front seat of the car for a moment before glancing at each other. Her father nodded once and her mother leaned out the window. "It's fine. Don't be too long, though. We're not unloading the car for you if that's what you're working at."

Cass forced a laugh and hoped it was convincing. "No, it's nothing like that. I really just want to have a look around my old hangouts on the way home." She pointed to the community recreation center just inside the gate where she'd spent a lot of time with her friends over the years.

Her mom looked where her daughter pointed and then back her way. "That makes sense. I think a few of your friends might even be around. Don't get distracted with idle chatter, though. You need to come straight home and help unload your things. You can find time to visit with people later."

Cass nodded as her father pulled the car onto the entrance pad and through the open gate into the community.

A quick check of the status bar one more time showed it was about 90% complete now. She needed to get through the gate before it closed again. She wasn't sure it would open if she approached after it closed. Her personal access code might not work anymore.

Cass started walking towards the gate and tried to time her approach so that she could slip through the closing barrier, but only after the system completed running the diagnostic update in her mind. She hoped that everything worked as planned or the security alerts would sound and the guards would arrive to find out who had breached the system and entered the enclave without permission.

She stepped through the gate just before it closed and stood inside on the pavement for a few seconds, taking a long, deep breath. Cass didn't know what the alert would be like but there were no sirens or alarms sounding. No security guards came running from the community center towards the gate to stop the interloper, either. A quick check of the *protocol one* file showed it pulsing a bright lime green color.

The upgrade installation had completed successfully. She activated a drop-down menu and saw there were a series of green checks next to the list of firewall breaches that the hacking program had made to allow her entry. She would have to check that list periodically to make sure the checkmarks remained in place or turned red to indicate a problem.

Cass set a reminder in her internal system to make sure she checked each morning to update the *protocol one* program in case it required any changes based on adjustments to the AI detection system. As long as she caught them quickly, Derek had assured her she would be able to bypass the system before it noticed her. She'd made it this far, but there was no guarantee she was going to be able to keep it up for the next month and a half. That worry, and everything she'd faced coming home, caused her stomach to roil as she started walking towards her house through the neighborhood.

Cass strolled past the community center but didn't enter. She spotted a few familiar cars in the lot, but she decided she didn't really want to see any of her friends right now. She continued down the street and turned the corner, heading back to her house.

She had a lot of thoughts spinning through her mind. Cass had slept the whole drive home, so she and her parents had not had a chance to talk about anything regarding school, or Shelby, or anything else. She knew that couldn't last. At some point, the topic of her relationship with Shelby was going to come up. Cass needed to figure out a way to bridge the gap between her family's feelings about Shelby's implants and accepting their daughter's relationship in some way, all while hiding her own cybernetics from them.

The whole thing felt disingenuous. Cass hated lying, which was probably why she was so bad at it. She was sure her parents would see through her deception immediately. The question was would they know what she was lying about? All these thoughts occupied her brain as she strolled down familiar streets.

Cass made a final turn into her part of the neighborhood. The house was at the end of the street in a small circular cul-de-sac. She'd almost reached her home when a voice called out to her from the house just before her own on the left. Cass recognized the voice immediately. It was one of her friends from high school.

Nick was the guy her parents had probably thought she would marry someday if she weren't gay. Though they accepted her homosexuality for the most part, they still kept inviting Nick over all through high school as if she'd change her mind or something.

Despite her parent's intentions, she and Nick became good friends, but that was all. They'd known each other since they were young. Their mothers had arranged play dates dating back to preschool. Nick was her best friend for the longest time until she met Susan in high school and the two girls began their relationship. When that happened, she and Nick sort of drifted apart. They still kept in contact with each other from time to time all through high school, though.

"Hey, Cassie, it's good to see you. My mom said something about you coming home today."

Cass smiled as the tall, dark-haired boy strolled down to the sidewalk through the grass of his front yard.

Nick pointed at her head after they exchanged a brief hug. "You look great. I like the new haircut."

Cass reached up and ran her fingers through her hair before jerking her hand back down when she realized she was lifting the hair away from where the skin patch covered her implant.

"Uh, yeah. I mean, thank you. I figured I needed a new 'do while I was away at school. It was time for a change."

Nick nodded and he changed the subject. "So, how was school in the big city? I always envied you a little for the way you broke away from the pack and decided not to attend one of the approved Sapiens college programs. That took a lot of guts."

"It was all right," Cass said. She wondered how much Nick knew about her time away at school. The enclave was a small, close-knit community. There weren't many secrets. "I met a few new people there. Honestly, I didn't have all that much in common with most of them."

"Nonsense, Cass. You can make friends with anyone."

"I used to think so, but it's awkward explaining where I come from to people who haven't lived here with us. That was probably the biggest challenge."

"You should come over to my house later once you get settled in back at home. We're having a bunch of the old gang over for burgers and hot dogs on the grill if the weather stays this warm. If not, we'll move the party inside. Since everyone is home from school for break, my mom thought it would be great to catch up and see what everybody's been up to."

Cass wasn't sure that was necessarily the real reason for the gathering at Nick's house. All of her friends had been away at school together the whole time she was away. The only one who needed to catch up on anything was her. She wondered if her mother had orchestrated this with Nick's mom. The two women were close friends and she wouldn't put it past her mom to use her friends to try and get information out of her daughter.

Cass tried to avoid committing to anything. "I'll see if I can come over. Honestly, I just finished exams and I might want to hang in my room a little bit."

Nick had a hard time hiding his disappointment. Cass spotted it right away. "Well, I hope you change your mind. It would be nice to have you over and I know everyone will want to see you."

Cass smiled. Maybe she'd misread the situation. "I'll see what I can do, Nick. Really, I just got home and need to settle in a bit first. I'll text you and let you know later this afternoon." She waved a quick goodbye as she turned back towards her house.

Nick stood for a little bit watching her go before he turned and headed back up the lawn to his place.

Cass cringed at the awkwardness of the encounter. Maybe she was wrong about the reason for the get-together. So many things had made her paranoid lately. She had a hard time trusting anyone since the events at the Sapiens rally when Shelby's brother was murdered. Cass realized she needed to find a way to push past that apprehension. She was home now. Things from back in the city couldn't touch her here.

Cass was lost in these thoughts as she walked up the driveway towards her house. Her parents stood at the back of the car, picking up a load of boxes from the trunk when she arrived.

"Good, you're here." Her mom pointed at the car as she lifted a small box that held Cass's make-up under one arm. "You can get the rest of the stuff. I need to go pull some things together for you and your sister for dinner tonight before your father and I get ready for our plans."

"Where are you going?" Cass asked.

"We have a dinner with some of the folks from Daddy's firm."

"Oh, well, Nick invited me over there for a cookout tonight. Maybe you won't have to make dinner after all."

"Really?" Her mom glanced at her husband. He grunted and took his load into the house. Cass's mother turned back to her. "That was nice of him. I think you should go."

"I was thinking about it. You and Dad go inside. I've got the rest of this stuff. Maybe Elena can come out and help me carry some of it, though?"

Her mom nodded and headed into the house.

Cass stood alone at the back of the car with the remainder of her things to take inside. She lifted a box from the trunk and turned to carry it up to her room. It was time to unpack and face life back in the enclave.

<hr>

Chapter 6

<hr>

CASS CARRIED the first box in through the kitchen, heading for the stairs leading up to her room. Elena, her fourteen-year-old sister, came bouncing out of the family room. She moved so quickly, she surprised and jostled Cass and she almost dropped the box.

"Hey, Cassie. Can I help you?"

"If you promise to slow down and not drop anything. You almost made me lose this load."

"I'm sorry. I'm excited you're home. I'll go grab something from the car. Is everything going up to your room?"

"Yes, but be careful."

"I will."

Elena disappeared outside through the kitchen door. Cass turned and went up to her room, putting the box on her bed. Her father had already brought the lone suitcase upstairs and laid it down on the floor at the foot of the bed. He was nowhere in sight, though. Cass turned and went back down to the car, passing Elena on the way there. She carried one of the clear plastic bins, this one full of clothes.

It took three trips between herself and Elena before they got everything stored away in her room. Cass couldn't believe how

40

much stuff she'd accumulated at college and that was after she'd left a lot in her dorm for when she returned for the next semester. Elena dug through one of the boxes with the extra clothes in it. She held out one of the University T-shirts.

"Hey, can I have this? My friends will be so jealous."

"If you want. I have another one that similar so that's okay."

"Supe!" Elena flipped the shirt up and over her shoulder and went back to searching through Cass's clothes.

It annoyed Cass how her fourteen-year-old sister pawed through her stuff. She didn't want to turn her away, though. She missed seeing her and felt like Elena might be her only ally in the house right now. Elena had been the only one who reacted decently when learning about Shelby and her cyber human status.

As if on cue, Elena pulled out a small photographic holocube. As she held it up and thumbed the switch, it displayed a short video of Cass and Shelby in an embrace beside a swimming pool.

Cass winced when she saw it. That was right before she'd had her injuries. She barely remembered when it was taken, since the accident had damaged some of her short-term memories. The implant had salvaged most of them, but the events of the few days leading up to that Caribbean vacation were all a little foggy.

"Awww, you two look so cute. Where was this? It looks like it was fun."

Cash shrugged. "It was. That was by the pool at the resort we went to for fall break."

"You don't talk about that very much. Mom and Dad remarked that they expected to hear so much more about it. I figured it was just because you didn't want to talk about Shelby a lot, especially after Dad found out about her."

"Yeah. It's something like that." Cass reached for the holocube. "Hey, put that down. I don't want Mom and Dad to see it."

Elena looked a little disappointed but put the holocube back in the box after shutting it off. "What's it like?"

"What's what like?" Cass asked.

"What's it like when she touches you with her metal arm?"

"It's part of her, just like her other arm. It's surprisingly warm to the touch and she can sense when you touch it, just like real skin. It's not at all cold and hard like you'd expect metal to be."

Cass watched as what could only be described as morbid fascination played across her little sister's face. She understood some of what Elena must be thinking. She'd had similar thoughts herself when she first met Shelby in person.

Cass grimaced as she considered the first time Shelby reached out towards her with her enhanced cybernetic arm. She'd flinched away from the hand as if it might infect her or something. It was strange how she'd become used to the caress from that arm in the time since then. Now Cass missed Shelby's touch more than anything else.

"In the beginning, when Shelby and I first met, I felt a little strange being around her. I wondered about the arm and everything we'd learned growing up here. When we first started seeing each other that way, I had to get over the feeling I had when she touched me."

"I'll bet. I wish I could've met her in person."

"It's not like she's dead or something, squirt. She just had to go home early last semester because of a death in the family. She'll be back next semester. Maybe you can meet her when Mom and Dad take me back to school. I figure that has to happen at some point."

"Oh..." Elena began, then stopped herself.

"What is it? You were going to say something."

"Look, I don't want you to hear something like this from me. Besides, Mom and Dad might've changed their minds."

"Changed their minds about what?"

"Cass, I don't want to say. You should talk to Daddy."

"Elena, tell me. Tell me now."

"Mom and Dad are not letting you go back to school. They're not sending you back there where you can be with her."

"They're not going to let me go?"

"I overheard them talking with someone about it over a face chat in Dad's office. I was in the other room so I couldn't see who they were talking to. I could hear what they said loud and clear, though."

"They can't make me stay here like I'm a prisoner."

"You know how Dad is. He's worried about you, Cass, and he wants to keep you close where he can keep an eye on you."

"I'm not a little baby. I can take care of myself."

Elena shrugged. "I think they weren't happy about you going away to begin with. Then, when they found out about Shelby, it just reinforced all the reasons why they didn't want you to go. What are you going to do if Dad doesn't pay for you to go back to college? You won't have anywhere to stay."

Cass shook her head. She couldn't believe this was happening. "That's not the point. They have to learn I'm an adult now. I have to live my life the way I want."

Cass didn't just worry about going back to school. She also considered how hard it would be to conceal her implant over the long term if she was kept here inside the enclave. It was bad enough she had to keep it from them for a month and a half during winter break. Considering doing that for the next year frightened her. There'd be no way to keep it from them. The synthetic skin patch would start to wear out. Frederick had told her she'd need a replacement eventually.

"Cassie, you have the most awful expression passing across your face. What's wrong?"

Cass turned away and walked over to her bedroom window, staring outside. "Nothing. I'm just angry at Mom and Dad. That's all."

Elena shrugged.

Cass didn't think her sister believed the excuse, but Elena didn't push the issue and let the subject drop.

Elena smiled and announced, "I got a new computer game. Do you want to come down and play with me? It's been scrubbed, so it has no net access for multiplayer, but all the good content is there. It's a fantasy game with dragons and swords and stuff."

Cass smiled. She and her sister used to enjoy playing those sorts of games on the computer together. The Sapiens Movement's programmers would purchase rights to new games and remove all of the game programming allowing access to the Mantle and the net that came standard with all games in the mid-twenty-first century. Once they'd done that, the movement would release a sanitized version to the enclave communities for the adults and children who played such things.

"I think that might be fun but I still have to put all this stuff away. Why don't you go down and play a little and I'll try to catch up with you later."

"Okay." Elena turned to leave but stopped at the doorway. "It's good to have you home, Cassie. I've missed you."

"I've missed you too, squirt."

Elena left Cass alone in her room. Cass continued putting away her clothes and other stuff she'd brought home from her dorm room. When she finished, she stacked the empty boxes and the suitcase in her closet.

Cass had spent the entire time she unpacked trying to figure out how to talk to her parents about going back to school. Elena was right about one thing. If Cass's father cut off tuition payments to the university, there was no way she could afford to go back on her own.

She hated the way that gave him control over her life and her ability to be with Shelby. It wasn't right that he did that because of Shelby's cybernetics. The problem was, Cass didn't know if there was a way she could keep him from holding it over her to control what she did.

The whole thing presented a problem for which she couldn't see a solution. The only thing she was sure of was that she couldn't stay here long term. Eventually, her skin patch would have to be replaced and who knew how long her hacking software would last before it had to be manually updated to keep her hidden from the enclave's firewall and security software. Cass didn't even know where she could go close to home to get anything like that fixed or updated. She was sure there was nothing like the Bizarre out here in the suburbs.

Cass thought about Shelby and wondered if it was possible for her to reach out and contact her from inside the enclave. She hadn't attempted to reach out to connect to the Mantle or anything outside via her implant since she'd arrived. Cass wasn't sure how much access she'd have in getting past the firewall's standard safeguards.

She realized right away when she opened up her connection that her access was severely limited from what she'd become used to over the recent weeks. Her implant could access fundamental parts of the old internet that still lay there hidden underneath it all, but Cass had no access to the Mantle system that gave her such freedom when she was at school. She hadn't realized how much she'd come to rely on it in such a short time. It felt like she was missing a part of herself.

After poking around in different access systems using her implant, Cass found she was able to send texts using one of them. She snapped off a message to Shelby to let her know she'd made it home safe and sound.

Shel, I'm back home. The software patch I got from the guy Frederick referred me to is working as far as I can tell. I think I'm going to miss you even more than I figured while I'm here. I am able to talk to Elena, at least. Maybe when the time is right, I'll tell her about me and my implants, too. Let me know how you are doing.

Love you, Cass.

Cass checked the message and mentally tapped the link to send it. As soon as she did, a message popped up with a red icon next to it. She ground her teeth.

Forbidden Address

Cass knew precisely what that meant, and it infuriated her. She stormed downstairs into her father's office. She opened the door and entered without knocking. She didn't know where her mother was, but she knew this had more of her father's fingerprints on it than anyone else.

Cass's father looked up from the tablet he was reading while working at his desk. He raised an eyebrow at her. "Yes?"

"You added Shelby's email to a list of forbidden addresses? I can't send her any messages."

"That's correct. Why are you surprised?"

"You can't do that. I'm an adult and I can talk to anyone I want to."

"Do you live in my house and inside this enclave? We have rules and those rules include not having regular contact with subs."

"Don't call her that."

"Why? That's what she is."

Cass refrained from saying something else. She wasn't going to change her father's mind on this. All she knew was she couldn't reach out to Shelby via the standard messaging system. Cass had promised her girlfriend she'd tell her that she got home all right. Shelby would be worried about her.

As she thought about that, another thought entered her mind. "Elena said something to me. She told me you and Mom weren't letting me go back to school next semester."

"She shouldn't have told you that."

"You don't deny it, then?"

Her dad shook his head as he answered. "No. Again, I ask you why you are surprised? I won't pay for you to go to a school where you've clearly come under the influence of a bad crowd."

"Shelby is not bad, Dad. She is just different."

"Those differences mean a lot to people like me. That used to mean a lot to you, too. That's how I know something's wrong. You never would have spent time with someone like that, especially not in that way, before you left home."

"You don't know what kind of person I'd spend time with, Dad. I have my own thoughts and opinions about things. While I agree with some of what you and Mom taught me, I've come to question others. Shelby, and people like her, have taught me that it's not all black and white."

"It is black and white, Cass. Those people aren't human. They mean to do nothing but create the downfall of humanity and they will do anything to achieve it. That includes corrupting young and impressionable minds who don't know enough to see through their deception."

"The only people I've seen so far out to harm anyone else are the people that associate with us here in the enclave."

"What are you talking about?"

"I'm talking about the video, Dad. I'm talking about the Saturday Massacre."

Her dad started to say something, then closed his mouth and stared at his daughter for a few seconds. He leaned forward, the expression in his eyes as hard as ice. "What do you know about that? As far as we can tell, that video was faked. It's not real. Nobody died during that rally. I have it on excellent authority from people who were there."

Cass realized she'd stepped into something here that was over her head. She couldn't let on that she knew anything or it would identify her as a potential source for the video.

She also knew all too well the video was authentic. People had died, including people she knew, at least in passing. As she thought about her father's reaction, Cass had the sudden realization her father knew the video was real, too. He was too highly placed in the movement for her to believe that he wasn't made aware after the fact of what went on at that rally.

Cass refused to believe he would've allowed it to happen if he had known ahead of time. Her father wasn't a monster. But he certainly would've been made aware of the truth, if only to help craft the follow up messaging for Sterling Noble and the rest of the Sapiens Movement leadership. That meant he was part of the cover-up to make it so people didn't believe in what the video clearly showed.

"We talked about it at school. A lot of us have seen the video, Dad. It's got to be real. How can you say it's fake?"

"I can say it's fake because I know people who were there. I know people who clearly say it never happened and will testify to that in a court of law. How come the police have been unable to turn up anyone who will say it happened or own up to recording that video?"

"Maybe they're afraid what happened in that video could happen to them."

Her father smiled and the look on his face sent a chill down Cass's spine. She needed to end this conversation before she said something she'd regret.

"Dad, we're not going to agree on this, I guess. I don't think it's faked, but I'm not going to change your mind, am I?"

"No, you're not. That is another reason you're not going back to that place. There used to be a time when you believed me when I told you something. Now, you only believe what you think you know rather than coming to me to ask about what's right and wrong like you used to."

Cass saw where he was going with this. She also knew that fighting with her father was the last thing that was going to help her get her way. She'd walked into this mess when she lost her temper about not being able to reach Shelby. Now she had to get herself out of it.

"I'm not the little girl I used to be. No matter what you do, I'll never be that girl again." She spun around and stalked out of the room, her mind whirling through scenarios and potential solutions to deal with this latest development.

If her father was complicit, even after the fact, with the Saturday Massacre, he wasn't the man she'd thought he was. This changed more than just a little girl's view of her parents. It might have turned her vacation at home into a prison sentence.

Chapter 7

ELENA SAT on the steps at the bottom of the stairs when Cass came around the corner from her father's office.

"That didn't go very well, did it?"

Cass jumped, surprised by Elena's presence sitting there. "How do you know what happened?"

"I can hear everything that goes on in Dad's office from my room. The vents in the air-conditioning go right past his office, I guess. If I sit over in the corner by the window next to the vent, I can hear him talking on the phone or with clients in person."

Cass had not been aware of this. Her sister had never shared that with her before.

Elena smiled and stood up from her perch on the steps. "I might be able to help you. I know someone who can get you past the firewall's security protocol."

Cass hesitated as she considered what her sister offered. How could she know something as sophisticated as this? Was it a trap? It was taking a big chance to trust her with something like this and if her parents found out about it somehow, they'd both be in trouble.

Cass decided to proceed slowly and see if she could find out what her sister was talking about. "How could you do that? You've never been one to fool with computers or coding much."

"My friend, Cadence."

Cass cocked her head to one side. She knew that name. "Little Cadence, with the braces?"

"She's not so little anymore. She's the same age as I am. Her dad took over managing the enclave's security systems earlier this year. She's been helping him and bragged to me the other day how she knows all his passwords and has been using them to watch some banned holovid programs that are not on the approved list."

"How do you know she'd help me with something like this?"

"Because I know who she likes and I'm the one who can get her a date with the guy she's been chasing since elementary school."

"How can you do that? Have you become a little matchmaker while I've been gone at school?"

"Let's just say I have my influence with some of the boys around the school. A few of them owe me a favor or two and I'm going to call those favors in to help you talk to Shelby whenever you want."

Cass wanted to reach out and hug Elena for helping, but something she'd said earlier made her stop. Cass stared at her little sister. "We need to go up to the room and talk, squirt. I need to ask you something and I don't think we should do it down here where Mom and Dad might walk in on us."

Elena shrugged. "Okay."

The two girls headed upstairs to their bedrooms. Cass opened her door and held it as Elena walked inside. Cass closed the door and tuned her enhanced auditory sensor to pay attention to any sounds coming from the hallway outside the door. That would alert her if their mother or father happened to pass by. It was nice having a computerized system in your head that could do things like that while you focused on other things.

"Why all the secrecy, Cassie?"

"You said boys owe you favors. I don't like how that sounds, Elena. You're not in some kind of trouble with them, are you?"

Elena laughed. "No, it's nothing like that. It's just that a bunch of them have liked me for a while now and I decided to see what that meant."

Cass bit her lip as she paused before proceeding. "Uh, squirt, you're not having sex with them?"

"And what if I am?"

"You're fourteen, Elena. Don't you think that's a little early for stuff like that? I was a lot older before Susan and I started fooling around."

"Look, Cassie, you haven't been here all semester. I've been able to handle things on my own without you looking over my shoulder the entire time. Don't worry. I've been taking precautions. The last time Mom had me at the doctor's office I talked to the nurse practitioner. She took care of giving me a shot that keeps me from getting pregnant and a vaccine to cover any kind of other problems."

"That's not the same as being ready for something like that emotionally. You're just a kid, Elena."

Cass realized she'd gone too far when Elena pursed her lips and her eyes narrowed. "I'm not too much of a kid to keep your secrets, Cassie. You're not gonna tell Mom, are you? You wouldn't do that to me."

Cass knew what the right answer was. She also knew she'd never be able to contact Shelby on her own without her sister's help. Maybe she could handle this another way. If Cass could get Elena to open up about what she was up to while simultaneously getting some sort of password through the firewall, she could solve both problems facing her.

Cass sighed. "No, I'm not going to tell Mom. But I do think we need to talk about this a little bit more in detail. I need to know what kind of things you're up to and make sure you're actually being safe. We need to make sure no one is taking advantage of you."

"How are you going to help with that? You're gay, Cass. You don't even like boys. How are you going to know what's right or wrong when dealing with them?"

"I know what's right or wrong. I had boys chase after me long enough to know what sort of thing they want and expect from a girl they like. You can't trust them, Elena. If you'll tell me about what's going on, I'll know if someone's not treating you the way they should. You shouldn't have to promise a boy something like sex just so I can hack my way through the enclave firewall. It's not worth it, Elena. That's for me to decide, not you."

Elena didn't answer right away. Then she nodded and smiled. "Don't worry. I'm not gonna have to promise anything. The boy I have in mind is harmless. He and I've just fooled around a little bit at a few parties. We've decided we're just friends. I think he'll go out on a date with Cadence if I just ask."

"All right, if that's all that's going to happen, then I'm all right with it, but we have to be careful. If her father finds out we're bypassing his security system, Dad will be more than just pissed."

"Don't worry, I've done this before. I don't think the same password will work as the one she gave me to watch the holodramas. Let me give her a call about how to bypass the messaging protocols. I should have an answer for you later this evening."

Cass nodded. This was taking a huge chance. Cadence had always seemed like a cute kid but Cass hardly knew her. She turned and opened her bedroom door to let Elena out.

Her sister stopped on the way out of Cass's room. "Will you tell me about what's going on with you and Shelby? I'd really like to know more about your relationship. She seems like she's very nice, but I'm worried about you, too, you know. She's totally different than anything or anyone you've brought home before."

Cass laughed a little. "I'll tell you some of it, squirt. The rest of it is private. Based on what I've just learned about you, I think you're old enough to understand what that means now, right?"

Elena nodded and smiled. She turned and left the room, heading towards the stairs to the first floor. Cass watched her go and then closed the door.

She sat down on the bed wondering what had happened here at home since she'd left. Her little sister had never been quite so brazen before. It was like she'd come out of her shell since Cass went away to college. Some of that was good. Cass liked seeing her sister be positive and upbeat rather than acting like the sullen fourteen-year-old she'd left behind when she went away to school.

All this talk of her experiences with boys, however, made Cass more than a little nervous. That kind of activity and acting out wasn't healthy and she needed to make sure Elena wasn't doing anything that could get her into trouble.

A voice called up from downstairs. It was her mother. "Cass, come down and help me bring groceries in. The delivery man is here with our weekly drop-off and I need your help."

Cass got up and headed downstairs to help her mother. She didn't know where her mother had disappeared to when she'd gotten home. Cass figured she had just gone back to her room to be by herself.

It was clear her mother wasn't happy with the way things were going with Cass and Shelby. It showed in little ways with her attitude towards her daughter over the last few weeks on the few face chat calls they'd had. Cass hoped by helping some at home, she could win her mother back to her side in all of this. She used to be Cass's biggest supporter in everything she did.

Cass called down from the top of the stairs as she left her room. "I'm on my way, Mom."

Chapter 8

CASS HELPED her mom around the house all afternoon. She put the groceries away and then offered to pick up in the living room and vacuum a little bit around the first floor.

Her mom didn't say anything. She just nodded and pointed towards the closet where the cleaning supplies and vacuum were kept.

Cass wasn't sure why her mother wouldn't say anything more to her, but figured maybe it was just going to take some time for her to come around. Now that Cass was home, her mother would have to open up at some point.

As Cass started picking up and got the old upright vacuum cleaner out of the closet, she discovered she was a little annoyed. Having lived outside the enclave for the better part of three and a half months, she'd seen first-hand the benefits of robotics at work.

At the college, the dorms were kept clean by robotic sweepers and vacuums. The machines did all the dusting, vacuuming, and floor maintenance all over the dorm. Here at home, they still had a device whose design dated back more than a century.

Cass chuckled to herself as she pulled it out of the closet from its docking station where it plugged in to recharge. She'd never known anything different before she went away and never really minded vacuuming before. Now that she knew some robots did every bit as good a job as she did, she wished she had the use of one here in the house. Of course, any kind of robot, even one with a rudimentary artificial intelligence on board, was forbidden. Because of that, she was stuck vacuuming the old-fashioned way.

Cass was returning the vacuum to the closet a few hours later, when Elena came around the corner and leaned up against the wall next to the closet door. An amused grin spread across her face.

"What's up?" Cass asked.

"Oh, nothing. I just talked to someone who shared some interesting information with me." Elena paused and looked around as if someone was listening in on their conversation. "Maybe you'd like to come upstairs? I'll tell you a little bit more about it in my room."

Cass realized that Elena was enjoying all of the cloak and dagger stuff but she went along with it because she was curious about what her sister was talking about. Maybe it was the code to call Shelby. "I'll meet you up in your room, all right?"

Elena nodded and took off upstairs.

Cass finished putting away the cleaning supplies and made sure the vacuum was fully docked in its charging station before she turned and headed up after her sister. She hoped it meant what she thought it did and Elena had found a way for her to reach out and talk with Shelby. She really needed her girlfriend right now.

Elena sat on her bed, tapping away at a game on her tablet when Cass walked in. Elena finished up what she was doing and nodded towards the door.

"Close it."

Cass closed the door and turned around. "Did you get it from her, the code for calling Shel?"

"Uh-huh. It was as easy as cake. She didn't even wait for me to finish the offer. She had it messaged to me before I could even give her Donny's phone number."

"You gave her Donny's number? You mean Nick's little brother?"

"Yeah, why?"

"Nothing, I just didn't realize it was someone I knew. I'm supposed to head over to Nick's later this evening to hang out with some of the friends who are back in town from school."

"Oh, you're going to the party Mom and Nick's mother set up for you."

"I wondered if that might be what was going on. I figured the two moms couldn't resist coming up with a way to try to get information about Shelby and me. I don't know what they think I'm going to tell my school friends that they don't already know?"

"You know how the whole mom network is. They have to be all up in our business all the time. Are you going to change your mind and stay at home?"

"No, I'm going anyway. It'll be fun to see everybody. I'll just make sure I don't say anything anyone could share back with their parents that might upset Mom and Dad."

"Be careful. I know a lot of your friends are worried about you, too."

"I will. So, what's the hack through the firewall? I want to reach out and get ahold of Shelby as soon as possible. I told her I'd let her know I got home safe and sound."

"I want to talk to her," Elena blurted out.

"Who? Shelby?"

"Yeah. That's my condition for giving you the hacked password. I want to talk some more to your girlfriend face to face. I want to know what the connection between the two of you is. I mean, I'm helping you hook up with her via an illegal Mantle connection. I figured that would be the least you could do for me."

"It's not illegal, squirt. It's just against the enclave's rules. There are millions of people out in the rest of the world that have no problem connecting at all."

"Fair enough, but you know what I mean. So, will you let us talk?"

"You mean like right now? You already talked with each other over face chat while I was back in college."

Elena crossed her arms. "I'll talk with her a little, then you can take your tablet back to your room and talk in private."

Cass realized she wasn't going to get out of this. Elena had made up her mind and it was probably harmless. "Fine. Give me the password and I'll make sure to let you chat with Shelby when she picks up."

Elena reached into her pocket and pulled out a folded piece of paper. There was a string of alphanumeric characters on it, twenty of them to be exact, according to her implant which had already cataloged the code to a port on the firewall as directed in the instructions. Cass glanced at it once more and put it in her pocket.

She pulled out her phone from her back pocket and opened up a connection.

Elena laughed. "You're going to need that paper, aren't you? Or did you develop a photographic memory while you were away at college?"

Cass stopped. She was halfway done tapping the twenty character sequence into the security system. She'd already accessed the hidden firewall port and started to open it with her implant.

"Um, yeah. I memorized it."

"You memorized it by looking at it for like two seconds? How did you do that?"

"Just a trick I learned at school. I learned how to remember things really fast because college courses are like that. You can test it. I'll show you what I have on my phone and you can see if it's the right one."

Cass pulled the folded paper out of her pocket and handed it to her sister while she finished typing in the password on the phone's virtual keypad. Cass turned the screen so her sister could see the sequence displayed there.

Elena looked back-and-forth between the paper and the screen several times then smiled. "That's awesome. You have to teach me that trick. It'll help me so much in high school."

"We'll see," Cass said. She was going to have to stall on that request. Short of putting an implant in her sister's brain, there was no way the kid was going to be able to replicate what Cass could do with her implant and cybernetic eye.

Cass looked over the connection through the firewall on her

phone and then double checked it using her implant's diagnostics. Everything seemed like it would work based on what she knew about such things. She noted that the *protocol one* file had lit up a brighter green color in her system folder indicating a clear connection to the Mantle outside the enclave. As she checked, a notification popped up in her head.

Outbound security protocol port open. Security override engaged.

"Hey, this is pretty good, Elena. I think it worked."

"Of course, it worked. She wouldn't dare give me a bad password. She knows I'd make her regret it til the day she died."

Cass didn't like the way her sister mentioned using mean girl tactics against her friend. She didn't want to make a big deal out of it right now, though. It was a little shocking at how mercenary Elena had become in just a few short months. Had she always been like this?

Cass tapped the send button, opening up a face chat session to the number that used to be on the firewall's forbidden address list. A few seconds later Shelby's face filled the screen.

"Oh my God, Cass, it's you. I wondered where that call was coming from. It was masked by some sort of security protocol. Is everything all right? I was worried when I didn't hear from you earlier."

"I'm fine, Shel."

Beside her, Elena cleared her throat.

"Shelby, you remember my little sister, Elena. She wanted to see you again and I thought maybe it would be an opportunity for her to kind of be on our side while I'm here at home."

Shelby's face brightened as she glanced to Cass's right. Elena had leaned in to make sure she was in the camera's pick up.

"Hi, Elena. It's good to see you again. How have you been? I assume you're still the only one in the family that's willing to help Cass out at home?"

"Oh, yeah, Dad is still supremely pissed. But I'm not like that. I can be open-minded like my sister."

"I'm glad to hear that. I hope maybe we can be friends, too. Do you think that's possible?"

"I would love that," Elena said. "It would be cool to be friends with you while you're dating my sister. I love being in on all the good gossip and stuff."

Shelby laughed at Elena's words, though they made Cass a little nervous. She figured it was worth the price to be able to talk to Shelby over the next month and a half while she figured out a way to get back to school.

"Okay Elena, you got to say hi. Now I'm going to go back to my room and talk to Shelby in private."

"Promise me you'll let me talk to her again sometime?"

"I promise. I'll check in with you before I head over to Nick's later."

"Sounds good. Bye, Shelby."

Shelby waved from her side of the screen. "Bye, kiddo."

Elena lay back on her bed, picked up her tablet, and began tapping away at her game again.

Cass held her phone out in front of her as she started towards the door. "I'm going to put you in my pocket for a second until I get back to my room. I don't want my parents knowing I'm talking to you."

"Why not?"

"I'll tell you in a minute." Cass put the face chat call on hold and slid the phone into her pocket while she headed around the corner to her room. She closed the door and walked over to the far side by the window before she tapped the phone to open the call again. Shelby smiled when the connection restored. "So why all the cloak and dagger stuff?"

"My dad had your connection information banned from our internal systems and firewall. I wasn't allowed to call you and couldn't get through."

"You're talking to me now. How did you do that?"

"It was Elena. She has a friend whose father runs security here at the enclave. She's been trading out passwords to other kids in exchange for favors at school and around the community."

"That sounds awfully mercenary for a fourteen-year-old."

"You have no idea. My sister's just as bad. Apparently, she's been trading favors with boys."

"Ewww, what sort of favors?"

"Those sorts of favors."

"I hope you had a talk with her."

"I did. I'm not sure how much good it did, though. She seems like she's enjoying being the top dog at school since I left. Dad's pretty highly placed in the movement and that gives her a certain amount of prestige. I used to have it, too, though I never abused the position the way she is."

"So, she's taking over as the reigning queen of the enclave?"

Cass laughed. "I was not the queen of the enclave, Shel."

"Oh, I bet you were. A gorgeous thing like you would be able to control all the boys even if they knew you were gay."

Cass blushed. "Shelby, it wasn't like that."

"But you think it's like that with your sister? Maybe she's just following in your footsteps and it's harmless."

"Unfortunately, I think it's way more than anything I did in that position. I just used it to get voted into student government. I think Elena's actually on the way to getting herself into some trouble. Hopefully, over the next month or so, I can figure out what she's into and how to get her to stop doing what she's doing."

"Be careful. If you let her in so she knows what you and I are up to, she could use it against you."

Cass shook her head. "She wouldn't do that. I think that's a line even she wouldn't cross. We're sisters, after all."

Shelby shrugged. She seemed doubtful, but didn't say anything more about it.

Cass let it drop and changed the subject. "How's your family?"

"Mom and Dad are doing well enough. I think it's going to take some time for them to get over Eric's death. I think it was good for me to be home with them, Cass. I know you didn't want me to leave when I did, but it was the right thing to do. Having me there gave them somebody else to take care of. It helped them focus on something other than paying attention to what happened with Eric."

"I wish I could be there with you. Anything is better than being stuck here with my parents. And it gets worse."

"How?"

"My dad says I'm not allowed to come back to school in the spring."

"Really? How can he do that?"

"Just like I told you before you left. He controls everything in our house. If he doesn't pay for my tuition, I don't know how I can come back to school."

"That's awful. We need to figure out something for you so that you can still go to school even if he doesn't help you anymore. There are scholarships and stuff like that you can apply for. I'll look into it for you."

Cass smiled. Shelby always had a positive outlook on things when Cass was down in the dumps. "That would be great. Honestly, I don't know what I'll do if I'm stuck here when the spring semester starts. There's no way I'm going to be able to hide everything from them that long."

"You'll be fine. Keep thinking positive thoughts. And don't do anything hasty. If you think you need to do something, try and reach out to me. We can talk through things before you get yourself backed into a corner."

Cass nodded. What Shelby said was on target. She was glad she had the chance to talk with her.

"Hey, Cass, I have to go and run some errands for my mom. I'll try and check in with you later."

"I'm not sure you'll be able to call me through the firewall. I'll tell you what. Leave a message for me on the school's server and I'll check that to know when you're back and when you can talk."

"That works. I'll leave a message there later and let you know when I'm home for the evening."

Cass smiled and leaned close to the camera's pick-up on her phone. "I love you."

"I love you, too."

Cass smiled as Shelby closed the connection from her side.

She sat down on the bed, realizing maybe things were looking up after all.

62

Chapter 9

AFTER HER CALL WITH SHELBY, Cass lay in her room on the bed while she did some investigating into what access she had using the password Elena got from Cadence. She found the port password not only gave her access to a communications link she could use to contact Shelby, but it also offered her access to a direct news feed from outside the enclave.

Cass scanned some of the stories, seeing if anything else had come of the call for investigations into the Saturday Massacre. One article talked about a conspiracy theory related to the Sapiens Movement's claims of a fake video. There were parts of the story that were shockingly close to the truth, including a link to the death of the man who had fallen from the roof near the rally at the time the recording was made.

Cass opened that story as she swallowed hard. She'd accidentally been involved with that man's death. The guilt about it still brought tears to her eyes from time to time when she least expected it. The article said a top investigative reporter was looking into rumors of someone else being on the roof with the man when he died. Cass wondered if this meant the reporter was getting closer to her and

Shelby. It wouldn't take much work to discover one of them had recorded the video and release their identities.

Her mother's voice startled Cass out of her focus on the news story. "Cass, I just got a call from Karen Glenn asking if you were coming over to the party there this evening? The weather's warm enough to hold it outside, but it will still be a bit chilly, and she wanted you to remember to dress appropriately so you wouldn't get cold standing around with your friends. They're going to build a bonfire, too. It sounds like fun."

Cass sighed. She knew what was behind the get together now and she didn't want to be questioned by everyone just so someone could race home and tell their parents about Cass and her freak of a girlfriend.

She walked down the hall to the top of the stairs. Her mother stood at the bottom looking up at her.

"Cass, you really should go. Everyone wants to see you. They're excited you're back home again."

"Mom, I don't feel like it. I just got home and it's been a long day."

"Well, I already told Karen that you'd at least pop over for something to eat for a little while. You don't have to stay long, but you really should show your face."

"Why? I can see them another time."

"You need to go because it's important to your father's standing in the community. There've been a lot of questions focused on him and his involvement with that situation in the city regarding that video. Then word got out about you and that girl."

"That girl has a name, Mom. Why can't you say it?"

Her mom ignored what Cass said. "It's important that our family show a united front. You have to go and that's it."

Cass realized she didn't have a choice. Her parents were going to hound her until she gave in and agreed to go. "Fine, I'll go. I'm not staying long, though."

"Just stay for an hour or so. I bet you'll be surprised at how much you've missed everyone. I'll let Karen know you'll be over soon. She and Chris are cooking burgers and hot dogs out on the grill for all you kids. Just relax and have fun."

Her mom left the bottom of the stairs, heading towards the kitchen.

The whole plan for the ambush party trapped Cass with no room to get out of it. Even if she somehow found a way to not go, her mother and the other moms would find a way to schedule something else. It was best to go now and get it over with. If she didn't give them any useful information, maybe they'd leave her alone.

Cass went back to her room and dug into the clothes in her dresser until she found an outfit she could wear that would be warm but also look good enough to avoid any catty chatter about her clothes. She was happy they could see her wearing current fashions. A lot of the parents didn't let their kids shop in those stores. Cass smiled as she looked at her outfit in the mirror. The jeans and blouse were casual, but made a statement. The sweater was both stylish and warm enough to ward off the night's chill. It was perfect.

Cass left her room and headed back downstairs. On her way past her sister's room, Elena called out through the open door to her.

"Hey, you heading over to Nick's?"

"Mom wants me to go. I really don't want to, but she's pushing me into it. She says it has something to do with helping Dad look good or something."

"Just go. You'll have fun and your friends probably just want to know what you've been up to."

"That's what I'm afraid of, you know that. The council of moms has spoken and have sent their kids to find out more about my life at school. I wouldn't put it past any of them to do that."

Elena shook her head. "You think all your friends would participate in something like that?"

"They would, if their mothers and fathers told them they were concerned about me and how Shelby had influenced me. Who knows what they've heard about me?"

Elena shrugged. "You have to go, so you might as well relax and have some fun. Maybe it won't be as bad as you think it is."

Cass nodded and continued downstairs. The advice wasn't all bad. She might enjoy talking with some of her friends. When she arrived in the kitchen, her mother and father were both at the counter working on something by the stove.

Her father looked up as she came through. "You look nice. Your mother tells me you're going over to the Glenn's for dinner and to hang out with your friends. I think that's a great idea."

"If you're worried about me embarrassing you, Dad, you don't have to. I'll be good."

Her father frowned. Cass realized she had sounded more than a little bit sarcastic and regretted it right away. She needed to get her father on her side if she was going to convince him to let her go back to school in the spring.

"Sorry, Dad, it's been a long day. I'm just going to hang out with my friends for a little bit. I won't be there too long. I'm tired and want to get some sleep."

"You have fun with your friends," her mom said. "I'm sure they're excited to hear about everything you've been up to."

Cass bit back a response. Her mother's statement seemed to prove her suspicions about who was behind the impromptu gathering. Instead, Cass smiled and nodded, then headed out the kitchen door to the driveway. She could hear music playing at the Glenn's house next door along with the murmur of many voices over her auditory implant.

The party had started without her. Maybe she was paranoid. Perhaps the Glenns were just having a cookout and invited Nick and Donny to have their friends over. Cass resigned herself to whatever she discovered next door and started across the broad swath of grass between the homes.

She didn't bother going around to the front door since the party was clearly in the back. Walking through the yard to the rear of the home, she saw a group of about twenty kids, all her age, hanging out around the patio and barbecue grill. All were chatting away.

Chris and Karen Glenn were by the grill, cooking burgers and hot dogs as promised. Karen took a platter of the burgers and dogs and carried them over to the picnic table. She set it down amidst the rest of the food which included some sort of pasta salad, fruit cock-tail, potato chips, and pretzels.

Mrs. Glenn looked up from where she stood over the table as Cass approached.

"Cassie, you decided to come. I'm so glad." She turned to her husband. "Chris, honey, look who's here?"

"Hi Cassie, welcome back."

"Thank you, Mr. Glenn. And thank you for having me over, both of you."

"Think nothing of it, dear," Mrs. Glenn said. "After all, you've had an open invitation to come over here and play since you were little. I know Nick and the others will be excited to see you."

As if on cue, Nick and a few of her other old school friends came over to greet her. Along with Nick were Meris and Natalie. They were two of her best friends from high school. The two girls rushed over and hugged Cass.

"Hey, Cassie," Natalie said. She was a short, dark-haired girl with a bubbly personality who always had a grin on her face. "It was so weird going away to school back in the Fall without you around. Still, you always were the one to be out in search of an adventure. I can't wait to hear what school in the big city was like."

"Yeah," Meris said. "It must've been full of excitement, espe-cially with everything that happened with that rally and all." Meris was tall with orange-red hair and lots of freckles. She'd gotten her hair cut short in a bob and it looked good that way.

Cass smiled despite the reference to the rally. "It's good to see you both. Meris, I love the new haircut. Did you get that done as soon as you left for school?"

"Yeah. Do you like it?" Meris primped at her hair with one hand while she turned around. "I figured it was time I started looking like a grown-up and get rid of that little girl ponytail I had forever."

Cass smiled and nodded. "Like I said, it looks great. I'll bet the boys all like it too?"

Natalie laughed. "She may have changed her hair, but the rest of her is still the same, Cass. She's still always on the prowl."

"Stop it," Meris said, laughing along with the others. "Just because I appreciate a good-looking guy doesn't mean there's anything wrong with that."

Cass laughed. "Nothing wrong with that, Meris, nothing at all. How was school for you guys?"

Natalie brushed her hand across her forehead as if she was wiping sweat away. "It's a lot harder than high school, that's for sure. You know I never liked school that much anyway and it was tough getting used to the different expectations from a university program."

Meris waved her hand dismissively. "You did fine. We were all there to help you out when you needed it. Don't let her fool you, Cass. Nat here found out she has quite the mind for advanced mathematics."

"Really?" Cass couldn't hide her surprise. Natalie had always struggled in school.

"Yeah, apparently I wasn't challenged enough in high school. Once one of the professors got ahold of me and put me through some testing, they figured out that I have an affinity for digging into computer algorithms. They fast tracked me into a security protocol major."

Cass pursed her lips and whistled. "Wow, Nat, I never would've pegged you to be a computer nerd."

"I know, right? The thing is, once I started working on it, I found out I really liked it. It's like I discovered a language at school I finally understand. We never studied computer code in high school so it was something completely new to me."

Nick stood by, letting the three girls catch up for a few minutes without saying anything. Then he cleared his throat to interrupt the chatter and pointed across the party. "There's someone else here to see you, Cass."

Cass followed his pointing finger and froze. Susan, her ex from high school, stood on the opposite side of the covered and winterized swimming pool staring right back at her. When Susan realized Cass had seen her, she smiled and waved.

Nick tapped Cass on the shoulder. "You should go see her. I

know she's been worried about you."

Cass shot Nick a glance. "Why would she be worried about me, Nick? That's a weird thing to say."

Nick shrugged and offered only an awkward smile at being called out like that. Both he and the two girls moved off towards another clump of Cass's friends nearby, leaving her standing alone between the pool and the grill.

Cass didn't have to worry about going over to Susan after all. Susan had already started around the pool in her direction. She smiled at Cass as she approached.

Susan came right over and pulled her ex-girlfriend into a warm embrace, saying, "Cassie, it's so good to see you again."

Cass hugged her back, then released the embrace as the two of them stepped away from each other. "It's good to see you too, Sue. How've you been?"

"I've been good. School has been fun and I got over being lonely after the first few weeks, once I started making other friends."

"I'm glad to hear that," Cass said. "I always wanted you to be happy after we broke up."

"You were right. We probably would've had a hard time keeping things going with you at a different school and all. I'm sorry if I left things awkward when we split up. It's been bothering me all semester that you might be angry with me."

"I'm not angry with you, Sue, not at all. I was the one who broke up with you, remember?"

Sue laughed. "Oh yeah, I remember. Really, though, I mean it. Don't worry about it. Seriously, I'm in a good place. How've you been while away at school? You're the one who didn't have any friends around you, after all."

Cass shrugged. "It wasn't that bad. It's pretty interesting seeing things from a different perspective than what we grew up with here in the enclave."

"Really?" Sue asked. "We all just went to another enclave with the same restrictions we've had here. You're the one who went out into the big bad world to learn new things. What's it like?"

Cass paused. She had to be careful here. This was likely what their parents would have told them to ask her about. "It's not all that different than here when you get right down to it. I mean there aren't all the restrictions on access to things over the net and there are different types of people than we're used to seeing, but in the end, it's just a bunch of kids going to school just like I think you guys ran into."

Susan smiled. "Yeah, but all those different people include some of those who might be considered dangerous to people like us."

The statement bothered Cass. The only danger she'd run into had been from Sapiens sympathizers. She bit her tongue and held off a sharp response, instead saying, "Really, no, I think most people are just like us at the end of the day. They just want to have a life and live it in peace."

There was an awkward pause for a few long seconds, before Susan smiled and said, "I met someone at school. She helped me get through things after we broke up."

"Really? That sounds wonderful."

"She's pretty awesome. She's from an enclave in the Midwest."

Cass smiled. "That makes me happy, Sue. I'm glad you were able to find someone new. What's her name?"

"Brenda. She's studying art history. She's hoping to start a museum of traditional artwork for Sapiens Movement members to visit when she goes home after finishing school."

"She sounds like she's great. I'm glad the two of you are happy."

"How about you, Cass? We all heard you found someone new, too. What's she like?"

Cass shot Sue a look. Cass's initial suspicions were correct. Her friends had all heard about Shelby. That probably meant they knew all about her by now. Still, Sue didn't seem to hold any hidden motives. She smiled at Cass and waited for her answer.

Cass decided to be honest and not hide anything. "Shelby's pretty awesome. I think she'd surprise all of you. She's nothing like you'd expect her to be."

Her diplomatic response surprised herself. She smiled at Susan and shrugged.

Cass didn't realize the other three had drifted back close to the two of them during the conversation.

Meris was the one who took the question to the next level, announcing their presence listening in nearby. "Cass, how can you say that she's normal when we all know she's not?"

Cass, caught by surprise, spun around to face Nick, Meris, and Natalie. "Why is she so different, Meris? Are you saying that because she's taller than me or has dark hair?"

Meris bristled at the confrontation. "You know exactly what I mean, Cass. We were all more than a bit shocked to find out you were dating a sub out there in the city."

Cass's temper flared. "Don't call her that. That's a name nobody uses out in the rest of the world. Shelby and others like her are people just like you and me. She's wonderful and one of the warmest people I've ever met. If you gave her half a chance, you'd find out you'd like her as much as you like me."

Meris snorted a laugh. "As if I'd even talk to her. I wouldn't let her bring her AI infected brain anywhere near me. I can't believe you let her touch you, Cass. It makes my skin crawl."

Cass was about to shoot off a sharp reply when Susan, of all people, jumped to her defense.

"Leave her alone, Meris. Cass did something adventurous all of us were afraid to do. She pushed back and found a way to get out of here, out from under the control of our parents and the movement. Even if it was only for a little while, she got out. We don't know anything about her girlfriend, only what we've been told by others who have their own agenda. We all know Cass. We should give her the benefit of the doubt and trust her instincts."

When she finished, Susan glanced at Cass, her eyes showing deep concern for her old girlfriend.

Cass smiled and nodded at the unexpected support, then said, "Susan, why don't you and I go and get something to eat. I think these others would probably like to stay here and talk to someone else. I know I am tired of talking with them right now."

She directed a level stare at Meris who, after a few seconds, looked away in embarrassment.

Susan smiled. "That's a great idea, Cass. Come on, I'm hungry too."

Cass and Susan left the other three standing there as they headed over to the picnic table where all the food was laid out.

Cass found herself at a loss for words once they were away from the others. "Susan, I…"

"You don't have to thank me, Cass. They were all being assholes. We all got instructions from our parents to ask you about certain things, especially about Shelby. I can't believe they went along with it. There was a time when all of us would've pushed back against telling our parents anything that went on in each other's lives."

Cass shook her head. She couldn't believe it either. "They're all probably afraid of what I might have become while away from home in the big evil city."

"That's crap. They're all afraid of what they haven't become. Look, Cass, I won't say I wasn't concerned when I first heard about Shelby."

Cass started a defensive reply but stopped when Susan held up her hand.

"Hear me out, Cassie. I know you better than any of them, maybe better than anyone but Shelby now. I know what kind of person you are. You never let anyone into your life who would hurt you. You're the best judge of character of anyone I know and I have to believe that didn't change just because you went away to school in the city. If you chose her, she must be a pretty awesome girl."

Cass knew how hard it must've been for Susan to say that. It meant a lot to her that she'd taken that leap of faith on her behalf.

Cass glanced behind her at the others. Most were looking in their direction. "I don't think I am going to be able to stay too much longer, especially if they're going to keep peppering me with questions like they did."

"They all have their marching orders from the council of moms."

Cass nodded. "Hey, maybe you and I can catch up some time alone where there aren't prying eyes and ears around. Besides, I'd like to hear more about Brenda. She sounds pretty neat, too."

"She's awesome and not as close-minded as you might expect from a mid-west enclave. You know, I wouldn't have had the strength to find someone new if it hadn't been for my relationship with you. I grew so much when we were together. You made me stronger and more confident than I ever thought I could be."

"We both owe each other a lot, Sue. I feel the same way about how loving you helped me grow up and learn more about myself, too."

Sue pulled Cass into an embrace holding her close and whispering in her ear. "Be careful, Cass. A lot is going on in the enclave right now. I don't think people are going to ease up on finding out what you've been up to."

She released Cass from the embrace and stepped back with a half-smile on her face.

Cass stared at her for a second, then returned the smile. She nodded and turned towards the grill a few feet away. Both Mr. and Mrs. Glenn were standing there talking. Cass walked over to them. "Mr. and Mrs. Glenn, thank you so much for inviting me to come over. It was nice having a quick visit, but I'm tired after the packing up and the trip home today. I think I'm going to go back to my house."

"Oh, I'm sorry to hear that, dear," Karen Glenn said. "Maybe we can have you back over another time when there aren't so many people here. I know Nick would like to catch up some more."

"I'd like that," Cass lied. She waved at Nick's parents and reached out to grasp Susan's hand one last time. Then, she turned and headed across the yard to her own house.

Cass felt like she'd just walked through a cave filled with vipers. She hoped she'd been able to avoid any lasting damage. Her response to Meris' harsh words was probably already being texted to all the moms in the enclave. Her own mother would be hearing about it soon enough.

Chapter 10

WHEN CASS GOT BACK to her house, her mother was still in the kitchen, now packing up the entree they were taking to their dinner engagement that evening.

Her mom glanced over her shoulder at the clock on the wall above the stove. "You're home early. Is everything all right?"

"Yeah. I was tired and decided to come home after talking to a few people. Everyone was great, but I figured I needed the rest. I'm going to catch up with a few of them another time."

"Well, that's nice. Did you get something to eat?"

"No, but I can find something for myself. You don't have to heat up anything special for me."

"Your father and I are leaving for the dinner party at the Connors'. The leftover food from what we're taking is still over there on the counter in the containers. Go ahead and make yourself a plate and heat it up. Make sure you put everything away in the fridge when you're finished."

Cass nodded at the same time her father called out from the front door. "Faye, we're going to be late."

As her mother left to go with her dad to their thing, Cass crossed over to the other side of the counter. Several plastic containers with leftovers from her mother's famous braised beef ribs and potatoes sat there by the fridge. She realized as her stomach growled how hungry she was.

Her implant required more than the typical number of calories to keep her blood sugar up and the cybernetics fueled. Cass was surprised at school when she had to increase the amount of food she usually ate. Since she'd been home, Cass hadn't had anything to eat at all and she realized she needed to get something now.

Cass grabbed a few remaining ribs from one of the containers and set them down on her plate. There were also roasted potatoes which she added as well. After she'd filled her plate with heaping portions of everything, Cass placed it in the microwave and set it to auto so it could reheat the food.

While she waited for the microwave to finish, she closed up the food containers and took them to the refrigerator for her mother. Cass waited until the microwave beeped, signaling her food was reheated. As she took the plate out of the microwave, she heard a chuckle from her sister across the room. Elena had come down from upstairs.

"What?" Cass asked with a rib held midway to her mouth.

"Nothing, I've just never seen you eat that much food at one time before."

"I guess I'm just hungry. It's been a long day."

"Yeah, but I haven't seen someone eat that much in a sitting since Cousin Mark was here for his football camp last summer."

Cass shrugged and sat down at the small breakfast table in the corner of the kitchen and started eating. She loved her mother's beef ribs and she realized how much she'd missed home cooked meals while away at college.

The closest she'd come had been when she and Shelby stayed with Shelby's brother Eric, while he recovered from his injuries while in police custody. She and Shelby had shopped and cooked for themselves while they were there. Still, it wasn't the same as being at home.

Cass looked up in surprise when her father walked into the kitchen. He wasn't alone. A short, squat man with blond hair and a scruffy beard followed him in.

Cass asked, "Dad, I thought you and Mom were going out?"

"I was until Aaron here stopped me out on the front lawn."

Elena gave the man half a wave from where she sat across from Cass at the kitchen table. "Hi, Mr. Benson. How's Cadence doing tonight?"

"She's home playing video games with Donny Glenn of all people. He called to ask if he could come over tonight."

Elena turned and winked at Cass as she said, "That's nice."

Cass's father held up a hand to stop the girls from saying anything else and turned back to Aaron. "I'm not sure what you were talking about out on the lawn, Aaron. Explain it to me again?"

"It's like this, Mr. Armstrong. Sometime this afternoon, around two, we had a major breach in our security system."

"But you said nothing was taken or scanned inside the system. You're saying someone just poked a hole of some sort in our firewall and then left, without adding a virus or anything like that to corrupt systems inside the enclave?"

Aaron shrugged. "It appears so, sir. It doesn't make any sense to me, but that's what happened."

"Cass, I don't think you know Mr. Benson. He was just telling me about a cyber attack on our security systems protecting the enclave. I think since you've been away, you've forgotten how we are constantly under attack from those who threaten what we believe in. We always need to protect ourselves from everything associated with the AI outside and anything or anyone connected to the Mantle."

Cass didn't have to guess what her father was talking about. It was clear he meant Shelby when he made that comment. Cass also knew it was most likely she and the hacking program installed in her implant that was responsible for the attack on the enclave's firewall that afternoon. She hoped they weren't able to track it down and find out it was her.

Cass turned to the newcomer. "It's nice to meet you, Mr. Benson. I think your daughter is a friend of Elena's."

"She is, and a good friend at that, aren't you, Elena?"

"I try, Mr. Benson."

Cass smiled at Elena and at Mr. Benson. "Did you figure out where the attack came from?"

He shook his head. "It's strange. It's from a wireless carrier of some sort that I've not seen before. It came close to the exterior of the enclave, but no one suspicious showed up on the surveillance systems at all, when we went back and checked on the recordings. We should have seen someone or something coming by the enclave's main entrance, but we didn't."

"So, you came over here to report it and stop me from my dinner event without having any answers? What do you think it could have been, Aaron? Something broke into our systems and you're saying they snuck up pretty close to our property to do it."

Aaron nodded. "That's how we designed the system. We wanted to catch anyone trying to hack in, by forcing them to approach the perimeter to run diagnostics on the firewall. We figured we'd be able to catch anyone that close to the perimeter and identify who they were before they had a chance to get away. This time, when we figured out what was happening, they were gone. I think perhaps they were either disguising themselves somehow, or perhaps using some sort of miniaturized remote drone that didn't register on our security cameras."

Her dad frowned and put a hand on the shorter man's shoulder. "I'm glad you brought this to my attention, Aaron. Please keep looking into it. There has to have been a reason for the break-in and hack. Please keep me up-to-date if you find out anything new."

"I will, Mr. Armstrong." He turned to Cass. "It was nice to meet you. I hope you enjoy your time home from school."

"I will. Thank you, Mr. Benson."

The short man nodded again to her father and then left through the kitchen door to the driveway outside.

Her dad glanced at his watch and then looked at Cass. "Your mother said you were home early. I thought there was a thing over at the Glenn's for you?"

"I was tired so I talked to a few of my friends and then decided to come home." Cass pointed to her nearly empty plate. "I guess I missed some of Mom's cooking for my first dinner back."

Her dad smiled. "Your mother's cooking is one of the things I like most about her. They say the way to a man's heart is through his stomach and she takes that seriously."

"Yeah, I think that works for children, too." Cass smiled at her father, despite her worry about how close she'd come to getting caught hacking the system that afternoon.

She finished up the last few bites before standing and carrying her plate to the sink. "When are you and Mom due home tonight?"

"We won't be too late. Now that I'm finished with what Aaron had to tell me, I'm ready to go back to the Connors' and catch up with your mother on the cocktails before dinner. She's probably already a glass of wine ahead of me, since I had to turn around and come back to deal with this firewall issue."

Cass struggled not to react and show the worry she felt inside. "I'm going upstairs and get some sleep. I've been up late studying for finals all week and I need some real rest in my own bed."

Her dad smiled and said, "Well, then, I hope to see you in the morning. Maybe you and I can sit down over breakfast tomorrow and try to get a fresh start on the day."

Cass knew that was her father's way of trying to straighten things out between the two of them. Both Elena and their mother were known for sleeping late when they could. Cass and her dad had always been early risers and often shared breakfast together when he worked at his home office.

"I'd like that, Daddy."

Her dad nodded, waved, and then left via the kitchen door, heading back through the neighborhood to the Connors' dinner event.

Cass cleaned up the rest of her dishes. Elena had returned upstairs to her room and was laying on her bed, listening to music on her headphones when Cass walked by on the way to her room. She decided not to interrupt her sister, instead going to her own bedroom and closing the door.

Cass hadn't lied to her father. She was exhausted. Partly, it was because she hadn't eaten much that day and her reserves were low. She was also emotionally tired from all the subterfuge associated with the day's various activities.

Cass's thoughts drifted back to the conversation with Mr. Benson in the kitchen. Somehow, they'd detected her implant breaking into the firewall before she could safely enter the enclave. She worried they might make some sort of a change to the system to try and detect her the next time she tried to update things.

She wondered if there was a way to localize her inside the enclave? If they could, they were going to discover her secret right away. Thinking the little IT security specialist hadn't had enough time to implement any significant updates himself, Cass decided to rerun the *protocol one* file before she went to sleep. Derek had told her after he installed it that the *protocol one* system would always update itself to keep her implant hidden from the sensors in the firewall.

The update in her implant pinged her right away with a notification of a change in the security system. Cass waited, sitting on the edge of her bed, fidgeting with her phone as she watched the status bar of her implant's readout in her mind continue to fill. It showed the program doing its job of resetting the system patch that hid her implants.

After fifteen very long seconds, the program finally finished running and the status bar turned green. Cass let out a sigh. She figured she was going to have to do this at least nightly to make sure she wasn't detected. She wished she could reach out to contact Derek about it but she didn't want to risk any unnecessary communications. As paranoid as he was, Derek probably wouldn't answer any calls from inside one of the enclaves anyway.

Cass lay back in her bed after turning out the lights and stared at the ceiling. She considered the implications of the frequent firewall updates on her ability to remain hidden. Aaron Benson didn't seem like he was the type to just let this intrusion in his system go without thoroughly investigating it.

As she lay there, Cass wondered who was better: her hacking

program installed by a short, little, paranoid, cyber human hiding out in an underground bunker or a short, little, paranoid technophobe hiding out inside a walled enclave. The thought of how similar the two of them were brought an unexpected smile to her face as she drifted off to sleep.

Chapter 11

CASS'S FEARS about another firewall update overnight were confirmed when she woke up the next morning to a chime from her internal notification system. The internal menu featured a red box framing the *protocol one* file.

She launched the program once again, letting it run through its system check. This time the status bar took much longer to fill and change from red to green. After several long minutes, it did change, though. Cass let out a sigh of relief. The prospect of having to go through this each morning wasn't appealing to her, but she had no other option.

This was only the first full day inside the enclave. Cass worried that at some point, Mr. Benson would release an update that would make it so she couldn't come or go from the gated community at all. Passing through the security wards at the outskirts of the compound would inevitably trigger something if her program was not perfectly tuned to the system. She'd have to be extra careful.

Cass reviewed the diagnostics file compiled when the *protocol one* program ran. Though she didn't understand much of what it said, she figured out based upon the documentation that updates were pushed out to the firewall first thing in the morning and occasionally just after dinner in the evening.

This information helped Cass to plan her days so that she could be alone in her room to focus on letting the updating program run, so no one would notice her zoning out to pay attention to what was happening inside her cerebral implant. It wasn't that she couldn't carry on a conversation with the hacking software running in the background. It was more that she became preoccupied with watching the notifications and queries scroll by as the status bar filled. She hoped it would give her some advance notice if a problem were encountered.

Even with the challenge of making time for updating her implant several times a day, Cass soon found herself in a familiar routine back home. Things seemed to relax a little between Cass and her parents, and she found herself enjoying the closer connection to Elena, as the days went by.

About two weeks after she got home, her father sat down at the family breakfast table and cleared his throat. "I'd like both of you girls to be around for dinner this evening. If you've made plans to go out with friends, you'll have to postpone them. We have a guest over this evening and I'd like him to meet all of you."

Cass shrugged. She'd been staying close to home and away from most of her friends, since the awkward barbecue party next door at the Glenn's on her first night.

Elena was another matter. She went out with friends nearly every night, even when she had school the next day. Cass's sister humphed and muttered something even Cass's enhanced auditory implant couldn't decipher.

Her dad put his fork down and stared at his youngest daughter. "What was that, Elena?"

"Nothing, Daddy. I was supposed to meet some friends tonight but I can tell them something came up."

"Excellent. Mr. Cantwell is a good friend who travels quite a bit in his work for the movement. He doesn't often get the chance for a nice family meal, and I want him to have the opportunity to get to meet you girls while he's here."

Her mom sipped at her tea and said, "It's been a while since Simon has been in the area. What brings him up this way?"

"He's handling a special project for Sterling that's extremely important. He needs to consult with me on a few things before he leaves again to continue following up on them."

"I'm glad Sterling has so much faith in you." Her mom turned to her daughters. "Girls, I don't know if you were aware of it, but Mr. Noble put your father in charge of tracking down the origins of that horrible faked video of those people dying. It's a huge honor."

Cass stiffened at the mention of the video. The original recording still sat stored inside her implant's memory system. She hadn't been aware her father was in charge of tracking down the recording's source.

Cass didn't know how much she worried about being found out, until she realized her hand trembled as she lifted a piece of sausage up to her mouth. She steadied herself and shoved the fork in her mouth, eating the sausage as she put the utensil down and placed her hands in her lap.

Surely she had nothing to worry about. Shelby had promised her she'd anonymized the video stream during the rally, so no one would know the video came from Cass's ocular implant. There wasn't a way to track them down, was there?

Cass needed to reach out to Shelby and make sure they were both taking whatever precautions they could to protect themselves from discovery.

Unfortunately, when she excused herself to head up to her room and message her girlfriend, her mother stopped her.

"Cass, while your sister is at school, I'm going to need you to help me get the house in order. It needs a good cleaning and dusting."

"I was heading up to my room for a bit, Mom. Can it wait?"

"No, there's a lot to get done before Mr. Cantwell arrives. He's an essential person in the movement and it's important we look our best when he arrives."

Her mom turned to her husband. "When is he expected to get here, dear?"

"Sometime around mid-afternoon. He wasn't sure when his flight was getting in. He's got the use of Sterling's private jet due to the importance of the project."

"Really, that isn't something I was aware of. This must be pretty serious business if that's the case."

Her father nodded. "It is. This video has the potential to topple the whole movement, Faye. We have to find those who created it, so we can discredit them and force them to own up to what they did."

Cass's stomach roiled as the discussion brought back memories she'd tried so hard to keep tamped down in her mind. Before she knew it, she was running for the bathroom in the hallway, overcome by a sudden bout of nausea as images of dying cyber humans filled her mind.

Five minutes later, a tap on the bathroom door made Cass pause as she wiped her mouth with a dampened towel. She stared at her face in the mirror as she asked, "Who is it?"

"Cassie, are you all right?"

It was her mother.

Cass bent down and rinsed her mouth again before answering. "I'm fine, Mom. I must have gotten a bad sausage or something. I'm sorry."

"It's all right. You just turned white as a sheet and rushed from the room. I wasn't sure if you needed anything."

"No, I think the worst has passed. I'll be out to help you clean up in a minute."

"That's good. Start in the kitchen with cleaning up breakfast. I'll help when I get back from dropping your sister at school."

Cass waited for her mother to leave with Elena before she came out of the bathroom. She'd been bothered by what she'd seen at the rally before, but never so violently. She hoped this wasn't something wrong with her implant and its interface with her brain. There was so much she didn't understand about how it managed her stored memories.

Cass wished she could take the time to talk with Shelby, but her mother would be angry if she weren't working on the kitchen when she got home in a few minutes. Cass settled for shooting off a quick text message as she got to work on the breakfast dishes.

Shel, my dad said there's a special project to track down the Saturday Massacre video. I don't know if there's anything you can do to protect us on your end but if there is, you'd better do it. I'll try and call you later when I learn more.

Love, Cass.

It took most of the day to get the house to the point that her mother declared the cleaning done. It turned out to be finished just in time. The doorbell rang fifteen minutes after the work was complete.

Cassie's father came out of his office off the main hallway and answered the door. Cass overheard a brief conversation with another male voice before the two men disappeared into her father's office. The new voice tickled a memory in the back of her mind but she couldn't understand why or place who it was.

Even though her father shut the door to his office, Cass could have dialed her auditory receptors up to pierce the simple wooden framing of their house and listen in. Her mother had other ideas of what she could be doing.

"Cassie, come help me get dinner ready in the kitchen. I might need to send you out to the enclave market for a few last-minute items."

"Coming, Mom." Cass glanced at the closed door to her dad's office as she passed by on the way to the kitchen. She knew they were discussing the video and wanted more than anything to hear what they were saying. Maybe she could find out more during dinner with some careful questions.

Soon dinner was ready and they started laying out food on the table.

"Cassie, go tell your father dinner is ready, please."

Cass nodded and walked across the hallway to her father's office door. She was about to rap on it when she overheard a comment from that strangely familiar voice. Once again, Cass tried to remember where she'd heard it before but couldn't place it.

"… I'm not sure how long it will take, but we've started to narrow down the possible sources of the video from the rally."

Cass's father answered. "That's good to know. You have no further information on who it could possibly be?"

"No, but we will. We've got our best people on it and they are tracking down every possibility. One potential lead has to do with the body of one of our followers found below the rooftop of a building near City Square. It appears the gentleman fell or was possibly pushed over the edge. The angle from that rooftop matches the recording angle of the video. We're looking into it."

Cass froze as she heard the words. They'd figured out where they'd stood when they'd recorded the video. That meant they could potentially track it back to the two of them if someone figured out they were up there. She had to warn Shelby. She might be in danger.

Cass tried to listen to more of the conversation. She was interrupted when Elena came around the corner.

"Hey, what are you doing? Mom told you to come to get Dad and his friend for dinner."

Without waiting for Cass to reply, Elena nudged in front of her and rapped on the door saying, "Daddy, dinner's ready."

"Be right there, sweetie."

Cass stood semi-frozen by the door, trying to decide what to do next with the information she'd overheard.

Elena stared at her. "What's come over you, Cass? You look pale as a sheet like you did at breakfast. Are you getting sick or something? Whatever it is, don't give it to me because I don't have time to deal with that."

Cass shook her head. "No, I'm fine. Just probably hungry, that's all."

"Good, I don't want you ruining dinner the way you did when we all had to listen to you barfing while we finished breakfast. Come on. Mom needs help putting the glasses on the table and filling them with water."

Cass followed her sister as she bounced down the hallway back to the kitchen. As she and Elena finished putting the last of the filled water glasses on the table, her dad entered the dining room followed by a tall gentleman with brown hair. His prominent nose should have made him memorable in Cass's mind, but she didn't recognize his face at all. It was strange because she was certain his voice was familiar in some way. Maybe she'd seen him in a news feed interview for the movement or something.

Her dad gestured to the guest. "Faye, Cass, Elena, this is my friend Simon Cantwell. I don't believe you three have met him before."

"No, I don't believe we have, though I've heard a great deal about you," Cass's mother said. She crossed the room extending her hand. "It's a pleasure to meet you, Simon. Welcome to our home."

Mr. Cantwell gestured around him. "It's a very nice home, Faye. I know how hard you work behind the scenes keeping things together so that James can do his important work. All of us appreciate that, though we probably don't tell you enough on occasions like this."

"It's nice to hear, no matter who it comes from," her mom said as she winked at her husband.

Her father gestured to Cass on the left side of the table. "This is my oldest daughter, Cassie. She recently attended the University in the city this past semester. Given everything that happened there, we are going to be changing her plans moving forward in the spring."

Cass's anger rose inside at the statement that she would not be staying at school. This was not the time to argue it, though. She forced a smile and extended her hand in greeting. "It's a pleasure to meet you, Mr. Cantwell. I hope you enjoy your dinner with us."

"I'm sure I will. I travel so much that I rarely get the opportunity to have a true home cooked meal. I'm looking forward to it."

Her dad turned to his right. "And this other young lady is our youngest daughter, Elena. She is just getting ready to enter high school next year."

"It's nice to meet you too, Elena."

"Yes, sir, Mr. Cantwell. It is nice to meet you as well."

Cass's father smiled now that the introductions were finished. "Shall we all have a seat?"

Cass took her seat on the far side of the table. Mr. Cantwell and her sister sat across from her, with her mom and dad on either end of the rectangular dining room set. As everyone started to pass the dishes around and began serving up the meal, Cass decided she needed to take a chance and try and get some information out of Mr. Cantwell. She needed to know more regarding the discussion she overheard in her father's office.

"I couldn't help but overhear you saying something earlier about a video and rally as Elena and I came to call you for dinner. Are you talking about that horrible video spread around everywhere about what happened at the rally?"

Simon raised his fork to make a point as he said, "What allegedly happened at the rally. And, yes, that is exactly why I'm here. How astute of you." As he finished speaking, Simon held her gaze for a little longer than was comfortable. Cass looked away first, pretending to be interested in something on her plate. She scooped up some mashed potatoes and shoved the fork in her mouth.

Her dad shot Cass a glance. "Cassidy, you know better than to listen outside my door."

Cass gulped down the mouthful of food. "It was an accident, Daddy. I was just walking over when I overheard what you both said. I didn't know if Mr. Cantwell knew I was at the University when that all happened."

Once again, Simon corrected Cass. "When someone faked a video of something happening, you mean."

"Of course, yes, that's what I mean."

Simon nodded and answered her before her father could object again to her intrusion outside his office. "We're working to find out who spread that vicious attack on our organization. I was telling your father that we are getting extremely close to narrowing down exactly who is responsible for recording and spreading that vicious video of lies."

Simon never took his eyes off of Cass as he spoke. A shiver of fear began deep inside her. Was it possible that he already knew it was Shelby and her on that rooftop? She had to believe he'd have told her father if he knew for sure. Perhaps that was why he was here in person. He wanted to talk to her face to face and find out if she knew anything.

Cass forced herself to play it cool. "I'm glad you're getting to the bottom of it. It really is horrible how things like that spread so quickly outside of the enclave. People out there seem to believe everything they see on the networks."

Her dad nodded and smiled at Cass's words. "That is exactly the problem, Cassie. It's all the more reason we need to get ahead of this and stay on the trail. No matter how many times Sterling denies the video's veracity to the news media, they still continue to spell out how their experts can find no falsehood in it. Despite the fact there were no bodies in the park and square after the rally, the reporters still insist it's true. The bodies they did discover have all been tied to drug overdoses and the like in a known user enforcement zone nearby."

Cass wanted to fight back and argue his points. She could deny everything her father said. She knew the truth. The drug overdose story and the cover-up that came out after the rally infuriated Cass.

The bodies of those killed in the video were all found in a dilapidated home in a rough part of town more than a mile away. Drug paraphernalia was scattered around them, even though all the families denied their loved ones used illicit drugs.

Still, it was a plausible enough explanation that allowed for the press and some of the public to start to doubt the video. It fed on a perception that cyber humans all used drugs and were involved in other dangerous counter-culture things.

There were still a few investigative reporters working the story and occasionally they put out articles and news reports. They never seemed to amount to anything though and the authorities mostly ignored them.

Cass kept her mouth shut and didn't say anything. If she had let out even a hint that pointed at her presence there, that was all her father and Mr. Cantwell would need to make the link to Shelby.

Cass had to finish dinner and get back to her room so she could access the hacked port through the firewall to contact Shelby and warn her. This all seemed to indicate their dinner guest was closer to solving this mystery than he let on. His mere presence here pointed to it.

Cass's mother changed the subject, asking Simon about how things were with some of the people they both knew at the national Sapiens Movement headquarters. The conversation shifted away from the video, for which Cass was thankful. Her mind raced through possible ways she could contact Shelby before the dinner was over, but she didn't want to get caught accessing her implant and sending a message while she was supposed to be paying attention at the table. She hadn't quite mastered doing two things at once like that yet.

As soon as dinner was over, Cass glanced at her mother. "May I be excused, please?"

"After you help clear the dishes and fill the dishwasher. Then you're welcome to do whatever you want as usual. You know the rules."

Cass stood and started clearing her plate and silverware first.

Simon stood as well and picked up his plate and glass. "Let me help. I don't get to do regular chores in a hotel room and I'd like to help out in exchange for this wonderful meal, Faye. Cassie, you don't mind if I help you clear the table and clean up a little bit, do you?"

"No, of course not. Help yourself."

Cass headed into the kitchen, setting her plate and glass in the sink before returning to the dining room to clear the rest of the dishes. Her mom corralled Elena to help out getting dessert together. It consisted of an apple pie and vanilla ice cream. The two of them worked in another part of the kitchen while Cass started rinsing the plates and putting them in the dishwasher.

Simon had taken off his sport coat and joined her at the sink. Reaching into the double-sided sink on Cass's side and pulling out one of the plates, he ran it under the faucet to rinse it off and handed it to her. After the first one, he stopped for a moment and unbuttoned his shirt sleeve, rolling it up to keep it from getting wet.

He picked up another plate to rinse it and Cass froze. There, on the inside of his arm, was a black tattoo of a clenched fist inside a circle.

All the memories flooded back to her at once and she realized where she'd heard Simon Cantwell's voice before. He wore the tattoo of the Sapiens First terrorist organization and he was the voice she'd recorded on that stage during the rally. Simon had killed Eric and all the others in cold blood and Cass had the video in her implant to prove it.

Chapter 12

CASS'S MIND RACED. She stood inches away from a cold-blooded killer. Her hands started shaking and she accidentally banged one of the ceramic plates against the side of the sink, chipping it.

"Damn."

Her mom turned around at the counter behind her. "What did you do?"

"I lost my grip on one of the plates, Mom. I'm sorry. I chipped the edge."

Simon turned around, holding his wet hands away from his shirt. "It's not her fault, Faye, I think I bumped her elbow when she was reaching for it."

"Accidents happen. Try to be more careful next time, Cass."

"Yes, Mom." Cass glanced to her side at Simon. He smiled down at her as he handed her another plate. Something about his grin unsettled her and it took her a moment before she realized what it was. The smile was genuine enough, but it didn't extend into his eyes at all. They appeared deadly serious, drilling into her as if staring through her to the depths of her soul.

Cass forced herself to return his gaze and took the plate from him. She turned away to place the plate in the dishwasher. She was almost finished. Just a few more dishes and she could retreat to her room and reach out to Shelby.

"Cass, I hope you don't run off once you're done cleaning up here," Simon said. "I'd really like to pick your brain about your experiences at the University. Your father tells me you met some fascinating and diverse people there."

It was no secret to whom he was referring. Simon had to know who Shelby was and she'd be willing to bet he'd made the connection to Eric, too.

A bitter chill replaced Cass's momentary fear as she answered. "Oh, I did. I'm sure it's nothing more unusual than what you've encountered in your travels, Mr. Cantwell. I don't think I would have anything to say that would be of interest to you."

"Oh, I don't know about that. I think you have all sorts of interesting things you'd be able to tell me."

"Simon is one of our best investigators, Cassie," Her dad said from the doorway to the dining room. "He's one of the leaders in helping us defend the movement from those that would slander us in the media. He makes it his business to know all about those people who might not see things the way we see them. That includes those from our movement who might have come in contact with them."

Simon smiled and nodded. "We don't need to beat around the bush, do we, Cass? I know it's an open secret among your parents and their friends here in the enclave. Your father already told me about your roommate. It must've been fascinating living in such close proximity to a s..." Simon stopped himself short of saying "Sub." He continued right away without missing a beat. "Let's use friendlier words right now and call her a cyber human."

Cass shot her father an angry glare. How could he have shared that with this man? "I am close friends with my roommate who does happen to have a few cyber enhancements, if that's what you're referring to, Mr. Cantwell. However, I really don't think there's anything you could learn from me that you haven't already learned in your travels."

Cass's mom turned around, holding the pie plate in one hand and a serving knife in the other. "I think we should all sit down and have dessert. You, too, Cassie. Perhaps this is enough talk about any subs."

Cass wanted to both shout at her mother for referring to Shelby that way, and thank her for trying to change the subject. It was even stranger when her mother glanced at her and gave Cass a bit of a smile, before she turned and carried the plate with the pie into the dining room. Elena glanced at Cass and shrugged before following her mother with the ice cream and scoop. Cass didn't want to remain behind to receive any more questions. She darted around the island countertop in the middle of the kitchen and into the dining room beyond.

The conversation shifted to general talk of sightseeing trips Simon had taken in his travels. Thankfully, they didn't revisit anything about Shelby during dessert, for which Cass was thankful.

She knew, however, it was only a matter of time before it came up again. She was more certain than ever that Simon had somehow connected Shelby to the video. Of course, it made sense. Her brother was one of the people in it.

Even though Simon was the one who put forth the cover story used to explain away the video, Cass knew he was aware of the truth. He also had the most significant reason to cover it up.

Cass sat back down at the dining room table and waited for her mother to serve up a slice of pie. Her father scooped a nice sized dip of ice cream on top of her slice and passed her the plate. Cass dug in immediately, staring down at the dessert as she ate, so as not to make eye contact with anyone else, especially Simon Cantwell.

After a bit of awkward silence, her mom asked their guest, "Simon, where are you staying?"

"I've got a place at one of the hotels by the airport."

"That's no good, right James? Why don't you stay here with us? You're probably tired of seeing the inside of nothing but hotel rooms with the way you travel around so much. We have a spare bedroom. That way you could have another home cooked meal for breakfast before you have to head back to the airport."

Simon smiled and nodded. "You know what, I've enjoyed

spending time with your family so much, I think that's a great idea. Are you okay with that, James?"

"Far be it from me to get in the way of my wife's hospitality, Simon. If she says you're staying, you're staying."

"Well, good. I have a layover for a couple of days and some work to get done. I don't suppose I could ask for a corner of that spare table and an extra chair in your office?"

Her dad offered a broad smile. "Of course, you can. You won't get in my way and we can talk about some things that we've needed to get done. This beats having a video conference anytime."

Cass kept eating. She wasn't paying attention to how fast she ate, though. Suddenly, Cass realized she'd started on the way to a monster brain freeze from eating the ice cream too fast. She winced and squinted at the sharp pain behind her eyes, especially the cybernetic one. It was worse because it seemed to travel straight into her implant. The pain caused her to gasp.

Her mom looked over at her. "Cass, honey, what is it?"

Cass put her hands to her head and rubbed at her temples. "Ugh, brain freeze."

Elena laughed out loud. "Serves you right, the way you were shoveling that food in. I can't believe all the food you've been eating lately, Cass. You are going to get fat if you keep doing that."

Cass lifted her head, trying to wait the brain freeze out as she squinted at her sister. "You let me worry about what I'm eating."

"She's right, Elena." Her mom shook an admonishing finger at her youngest daughter. "I think Cass has done a great job with eating while away at school. It doesn't look like she's gained the typical freshman fifteen at all. Considering how all her friends looked when they came back from campus, I think that's an accomplishment."

Cass smiled at her mom's comment. The brain freeze headache started to fade. Gaining weight at school wasn't an issue for her. That was one advantage to having cybernetic implants that ran off of the body's blood sugar supply. She didn't know many cyber humans who were overweight.

Cass slid her chair back from the table. "Mom, can I be excused? I think I need to lay down until this headache goes away."

"Of course, dear. We'll clean-up for you. I hope you feel better?"

Cass got up. "I will. Thanks, Mom." Cass left the table. She made sure not to glance in Simon's direction as she walked into the hallway.

Running up the stairs once she was out of sight, Cass turned the corner in the upstairs hall towards her room. As soon as she was inside, she shut the door and headed for the bed. She needed to get in touch with Shelby right away. The brain freeze headache had provided the perfect excuse for her getting away from the table and the awkward discussion about the events at the rally and the viral video.

Cass started to send the message without thinking to check the *protocol one* file to make sure the firewall hadn't updated after dinner. She realized her error too late as the text started to go out.

In an instant, there was a flurry of alarms inside her head. The *protocol one* file opened on its own and began running in the background. She noticed it and then saw the warning message coming across her visual field right next to it.

Emergency disconnection protocol in place.
Firewall counter-penetration activity detected.
Recommendation: Remain off-line until the update is completed.

Cass cursed. How was she supposed to warn Shelby if her implant was now flagged by the firewall because she hadn't been paying attention? Cass watched the *protocol one* file running in the background. Its icon flashed a glowing neon red as the status bar took much longer to cycle through its process this time around. Clearly, she'd triggered some kind of security response and now was paying the price for it.

Cass disconnected everything she could, but the access point used by the *protocol one* hacking system, and sat back in bed. What was she going to do? She had to warn Shelby somehow.

Cass went over and tried her tablet from school. Unfortunately, it was tied to her implant now. Shelby had helped her hack that system back at school so she could still use it to study in tandem with her enhancements. The device had her identifier code in it. While the code was anonymous, it was the same as her implant and now the tablet was unable to make the connection outside the enclave either.

There had to be a way to get past all of this. She had to work around it somehow.

Cass got up and paced around her room, pondering the problem, when there was a tap at her door.

"Who is it?"

"It's me, Sis."

Cass sighed. "Come in."

"What's wrong, Cass?" Elena nodded at the tablet on the desktop, its screen displaying a non-connection icon. "Are you going to try to call Shelby?"

"Yeah, but my tablet's updating and I can't get it to access anything outside the firewall." An idea popped into Cass's head. "Do you think I could use your tablet to call her?"

Elena smiled. "Of course, but you have to let me say hi."

"You can if you want." Cass rubbed the side of her head, trying to make the remainder of the headache go away. As she did, Elena gasped.

"Cassie, what's wrong with your face?"

Cass froze, her hand flattening against the side of her cheek, feeling the place where the skin patch that covered her implant had lifted away where she'd been rubbing at her head.

"Oh, it's nothing. Just a scab. I've got a bruise there I bumped into something this morning. I put some makeup on it until it fades." Cass tried to turn away as her sister came closer, leaning in towards her face.

"Cassie, that's not a scab. I saw something shiny." Elena's hand covered her mouth. "Oh my God, Cass. You've got an implant."

Elena started to turn for the door.

Cass ran past her and closed it, standing with her back to the entrance so that Elena couldn't leave. "Elena, you have to understand what happened. I was in a horrible accident and when I woke up, the doctors used it to fix what was wrong with me. I didn't do it on purpose. I swear."

"I can't believe this. You're a sub, now, just like Shelby."

"Don't call me that. Don't call any of us that. I just told you, I didn't do it on purpose. It was done to me by doctors to save my life. I'm still your sister. I'm still me, see? There's nothing different."

There was a long pause as the two sisters stared at each other. For a second, Cass feared her sister might scream or call out or something. Her mind whirled through possible ways she could keep her sister quiet until she could get away.

Elena reached up towards Cass's face with her fingertips. "Can I see you?"

"What? You just saw."

"Please, Cassie?"

Cass reached up and pressed at the magnetized points where the skin patch attached to her face. The edges lifted up from the nearly perfect seam it made with her actual skin. As she peeled the flap of synthetic skin away and took her hand from the side of her face, Elena gasped again.

"Whoa, Cass, that is so weird. Did it hurt when you got it?"

Cass shrugged. "I was unconscious. I don't remember. I woke up in the hospital, after I was in a bad jet ski accident on my fall break trip to the Caribbean. The doctors down there on the island said my brain was so badly injured that this was the only way they could save my life."

"So, you don't have superpowers or anything like that?"

Cass shook her head. "Nope, just the implant there, oh, and my eye and ear, too."

Elena took a step forward, leaning in closer. "Your eye? But it looks just like your real eye. You're messing with me."

"No, I'm not. Keep watching my right eye and I'll prove it to you."

Cass concentrated, activating a decorative feature built into her ocular implant. She never used it in public. As Cass enabled the function, the iris of her eye changed color and glowed with a deep blue around her pupil.

"Oh, my God, you're right. You've got a fake eye. Can you see out of it?"

Cass smiled. "Of course, I can. It's actually better than my real eye was. I can see things and even zoom in to things far away. I can also see in the dark without having any lights on."

Elena went back to studying the metal implant in the side of Cass's face. Her fingers probed gently around her sister's cheek. "What are you going to do when Mom and Dad find out?"

"They're not going to find out, Elena. I'm not telling them and neither are you."

"You're not going to be able to hide it from them forever, Cassie. Eventually, they'll find out about it. They figure out everything we try to get away with." Elena paused, as she went back to studying her sister's face. "Hey, how did you get into the enclave in the first place? Aren't they supposed to keep anyone with cybernetic implants out?"

Cass shrugged. "Actually, I used a friend of Shelby's to help me find a guy who could get through the firewall. He wrote a program to help me and installed it so that I could fool the system while I was staying here."

Elena snapped her fingers. "Wait a minute. You're the reason Cadence's father is pulling his hair out. She's been telling me how he's been running around trying to figure out who's been hacking into the enclave's system every day. Every time he updates something, the system gets hacked again and he doesn't know how it's happening."

Cass didn't say anything. She realized she'd already said too much. "Look, Elena, I just wanna talk to Shelby." She gestured at her face. "And I need you to keep this a secret just between you and me, okay?"

Elena smiled. "Don't worry. Your secret is safe with me. I want to hear more about what you can do, though. You haven't even told me about your super ear."

Cass winced at the description. "Look, I'll tell you all about anything you want to know later. Now, I just want to talk to Shelby a little bit. When I'm done, I'll come by your room and we can talk some more. Go get your tablet and bring it back to me, while I put this back on my face, before someone comes in the room and sees me."

Cass went over to her mirror and started to replace the skin patch while Elena left the room, pulling the door shut behind her. Cass made sure the seals were in place and the dermal adhesive had attached all the way around the patch, then stepped back from the mirror, examining her work.

Her face looked normal again. Cass ran her fingers through her hair to make sure it hung down over her cheek, just in case something peeled up again. Frederick had told her when she bought the patch that it wasn't permanent. She realized the attachment points were weakening the more she used it and eventually she'd have to get it replaced. How she was going to do that while stuck here in the enclave, Cass didn't know.

She sat down on the bed and waited for Elena to come back with the tablet so she could call Shelby. There was so much she had to tell her girlfriend. So much had happened and Cass wasn't sure what would happen next. It all frightened her.

Chapter 13

SHELBY MOORE SAT BACK and relaxed as her parents' automated car navigated the way home from the market. Her mother and father had sent her out for groceries after dinner while they cleaned up. They planned on watching a holovid together as a family when Shelby returned.

Enjoying the alone time on the drive back from the store, Shelby had a moment to think about how different life at home was since she'd left school. Her parents' grief reflected her own, though hers was compounded by having witnessed her brother's death. She was unable to share that fact with anyone, even her mother and father, which intensified the trauma for her.

Shelby missed Eric, too. The weeks since he'd been killed had been hard on her whole family, as they tried to understand and deal with the void in their lives his death had created. An additional difficulty for Shelby came from her separation from Cass. Not having Cass here to lift her up with her infectious laugh made the somber mood in the Moore home hard to bear.

Cass hadn't called for several days and Shelby hoped they'd be able to connect tonight. As if on cue, the incoming call alert sounded over her cerebral implant. Shelby's excitement that it might be Cass dampened when she saw it was a face chat call from a strange number. Shelby was already connected to the car's systems, so she leaned forward and tapped a button on the dash to deploy a small remote camera and holo-screen. As the screen popped up in front of her, she was surprised to see Cassie's face fill the screen.

"Cass, I didn't know it was you. Is this a new number?"

"No, I'm using my sister's tablet. The firewall here flagged my system tonight and is searching for me on the network. I'm trying to get the *protocol one* program to work so I can hide again. Until then, I have to stay off the grid completely. That's why I am using Elena's tablet."

Shelby smiled when another face popped into the screen beside Cass. "Hi Shelby, remember me?"

"Yes. Of course, I do. How are you, Elena?"

"Oh, I'm fine. Cass here just showed me her implant and all. She even made her eye glow for me. It's really cool."

Shelby grew concerned and glanced towards Cass through the video pick up. "Cass, are you all right? You're not in any kind of trouble, are you?"

"No, Shel, I'm fine. I happened to let it slip when my skin patch started to peel away and Elena spotted it. She's all right though, aren't you, squirt?"

"Yeah, it's the best secret in the world. I can't believe I'm the only kid around whose sister is a… um, cyber human."

Shelby knew Elena had almost said the word sub out of reflex before she'd stopped herself. That was all right, though. Elena had stopped herself before she said it and sometimes habits like that were hard to break.

Shelby worried that Cass's secret had slipped so soon, but discovery by the enclave's security firewall was a much bigger concern. "You said they somehow caught you getting through the firewall?"

Cass nodded. "It was my own dumb fault. I was in such a hurry to call you that I didn't remember to check the firewall for updates first. I opened the connection before I realized they were watching for a breach."

"How serious is it, Cass? If you need to leave, I can try to come down there."

Cass shook her head. "No, it's fine. I shut down my implant's wireless systems and broke contact. There shouldn't be any way to trace me now that I've powered down."

Shelby let out a sigh of relief. "You need to be more careful, Cassie."

"I will." Cass glanced at her sister, still sitting next to her, giving her a little nudge with her shoulder.

Elena smiled. "Oh, yeah, you two want some private time, don't you?"

Shelby laughed. The way Elena had said it made Cass blush and scowl at her sister.

Cass pointed towards the door. "You can leave now, Elena. I'll bring you your tablet when we're finished."

"I'm leaving. You can bring it to me in the morning if it's too late. That's fine." Elena waved at Shelby and left the room.

Shelby watched the fourteen-year-old leave and pull the door closed in the background behind Cass.

Cass waited until her sister left, glancing over her shoulder to be sure the door was shut before she continued, urgency coloring her tone. "Shelby, listen to me. I think you might be in danger."

"What are you talking about? I'm fine. I just came from the market to pick up some groceries. I'm heading towards my parents' house now."

Cass shook her head. "No, you need to listen to me. This is serious. There's a man here visiting my father. I recognized him, Shel. He's… he's the man from the stage at the rally. The one who killed Eric and the others. I recognized his voice right away and he has the same tattoo on his arm. It's the same guy."

Shelby froze at Cass's words. She wanted to scream in a combination of rage, sorrow, and joy all at once. She'd been fantasizing about all the ways she wanted to kill that man if she ever discovered his identity. Now, she found out he was visiting Cass's home as a family guest.

A chill fell over Shelby's voice. "What's his name?"

"Simon Cantwell. Dad called him a troubleshooter for the movement. The tattoo on his arm makes him a member of the Sapiens First militants."

"Has he let on that he knows you recorded the video? How do you know I'm in danger?"

"He was talking to my father. He's helping the movement track down the origin of the video and they found a link between the man I pushed off the roof and the location where it was recorded."

"You didn't push the man off the roof, Cass. He fell off all on his own. I was there, remember? Besides which, he was going to turn us in. Who knows what would've happened to us if he did that?"

Cass shook her head. "That's doesn't matter now."

She glanced over her shoulder at the bedroom door once again then back at the screen. "Shel, I think he knows it was us. He just said some things to me after dinner that led me to believe he knows all about you and I being together and he's tied the fact that Eric's your brother to the release of the video."

Shelby paused for a second, her mind whirling through possible scenarios. If Cass was right, she wouldn't put it past those bastards to come looking for her. They'd already proven they were willing to kill for their twisted beliefs. What would she do if they came for her?

"Look, Shelby, is there someplace you can go? Someplace that's safe where no one will know where you are?"

"I have a cousin that lives back down your way. We haven't visited or even talked to her in a long time, but that's probably a good thing."

"I think you should go visit her, Shel. I think you should go really soon."

"Cass, everything here is fine."

"Shelby, you need to trust me. I have a really horrible feeling about all of this. I don't know how, I just know that something bad is about to happen and Simon Cantwell is behind it. He was too smug in the way he talked to me."

Shelby tried to come up with another excuse. She was sure Cass was overreacting. Just as she was about to answer her girlfriend's concerns, the automated car turned the corner onto the street to Shelby's home. That was when she saw the first of the blue flashing strobes of police vehicles. There were several police cars parked out in front of her house. Some of them blocked the street ahead.

"Oh, my God. Cass, I have to go."

"What's wrong?"

"There are police all around my house. Something is wrong."

"No, Shelby. You can't trust anyone. You need to leave. Now. Just keep on driving past and don't stop. Remember how we got locked up before. The police could be in on it."

"Cass, the police aren't all corrupt. This is another state, another city. Just because the police chief back there was working with your father, doesn't mean all the police are bad."

"Shelby. You have to listen to me. I don't know how I know it, but this is all wrong. Somehow what's happening at your house is related to Simon being here at mine."

Shelby reached out to touch the button next to the screen that would cut the connection off.

"Cass, I have to stop. I have to know what's going on with my parents."

"Shelby, please don't."

"I have to. Don't worry, I'll be careful." Shelby tapped the virtual screen and closed the holographic window. The car was already slowing as it approached the emergency vehicles filling the street ahead.

She could tell the automated robotic driver was perplexed by the jumble of vehicles arrayed in front of it. Shelby reached out through her implant, activating the connection to communicate with the car.

She spoke aloud. "Pull over here and wait. I'll walk the rest of the way."

"Very well," the disembodied voice of the robotic car said.

The car pulled to the curb and Shelby climbed out. As she

exited the vehicle, the automated voice spoke again. "I detect items in the storage compartment. Do you need them? I can open the trunk for you."

"No, leave them there. I'll be right back." Shelby started to walk down the street towards her house. She resisted the urge to run, remembering what Cass had told her. She took the warning to heart and opted to be cautious. The last time Cass had a bad feeling about something, Erik had died.

Shelby almost reached the sidewalk in front of her neighbor's home, when a police officer standing on the lawn nearby turned and came over to stop her.

"Sorry, Miss. You can't come through here."

"What's the problem, officer?" Shelby asked.

The uniformed woman hooked a thumb over her shoulder at Shelby's home. "There's been a situation in this house behind me. I don't know all the details, but we've been told to cordon off this part of the neighborhood for now."

Shelby nodded as she glanced past the officer at the collection of vehicles. There were four police cars with blue and red light-bars on top, lit up and flashing their strobes into the night's darkness.

Next to the marked police vehicles, there was also a larger black van pulled up in front of the police cars by the driveway. It, too, had a flashing light-bar but this one was not on the roof. It was sitting on the dash inside so it flashed out the front window.

Shelby hid a gasp, turning it into a fake cough when she saw a familiar emblem on the van's rear window. There was a small, black sticker of a white circle with a black clenched fist inside it.

She looked away and back at the officer as soon as she spotted it. That van belonged to Sapiens First or at least belonged to a police officer who sympathized with the militants. Cass was right. The police here near Boston, or at least some of them, were working with the terrorists who'd killed her brother.

The female officer in front of Shelby pointed back up the street. "Look, Miss, I'm going to have to ask you to go back to your car. Do you live on this street somewhere or are you just passing through?"

Shelby's mind spun with possible responses. "Um, yeah... I

mean, no, I don't live here. I was using this street as a shortcut home from the market. I live a few streets over that way."

"Well, you'd better turn around and go back the long way. I have a feeling this street's going to be closed for some time, while they bring the bodies out."

Shelby halted in the middle of her turn to go back to the car. Her mind spun through the possibilities based on what the officer said. She resisted the urge to ask another question.

With the mention of bodies in her home, Shelby knew right away that the Sapiens First team disguised as police had killed her parents. There was no way her elderly parents had killed anyone and that meant only one thing.

Shelby wanted to scream, to cry, to do anything but turn around and leave. She knew she could do none of those things. They'd capture and kill her as well if they discovered who she was.

"Thank you, officer." Shelby hoped the police woman couldn't detect the quaver in her voice. "I'll go back and turn around like you said. I hope you catch whoever did this."

The woman didn't answer Shelby. She merely nodded and watched as the girl turned and headed back towards the automobile. The door popped open automatically as Shelby approached, recognizing her implant.

Shelby climbed in and sat down in the seat behind the steering wheel. Her mind was numb with grief. The dashboard controls lit up as she somehow managed to reach out to turn on the engine. The fully electric vehicle had been completely charged when she had left the house.

Shelby knew she had to get away. There was no time to grieve. She double-checked the readout on the dash through the blur of her tears. She had to make sure she had enough of a charge to get away from the Boston area before she stopped again.

Shelby entered a waypoint on the interstate south of Boston and engaged the autopilot. It wasn't going to take long for that officer to talk to someone who knew more of what was going on. When that happened, she'd realize the girl who'd left in the car lived in that house. Shelby had to be far away by the time that happened.

She turned and looked out the back window to see if anyone was following her as the car headed back up the street towards the market. This time, though, it continued past the store, driving towards the interstate. Shelby had only been half kidding about going to visit her odd cousin in Pennsylvania. Now, that distant cousin seemed to be the only family Shelby had left.

Chapter 14

A FEW MINUTES LATER, as Shelby's car pulled onto the interstate heading south, she pondered her options. She was now officially on the run. She had to assume the Sapiens First thugs would be tracking her any way they could.

It was a struggle to organize her thoughts. She kept spinning back to trying to picture her parents. Why couldn't she see their faces?

Shelby shook her head, her hands clenched into fists. "Get your act together, or you're going to end up dead like everyone else in your family."

Shelby went down the list of things she'd done to escape so far. She'd already disconnected her personal cerebral implant's interface and unique identifier from the Mantle. Even though those people weren't supposed to be able to use the Mantle in that way, she wouldn't put anything past them in the accomplishment of their organization's goals.

She'd also started the car on the road south. Her initial plan to head south to visit her cousin, Ramona Roche, was based in part on the fact that Ramona was known in the family as a pretty decent hacker. She'd always bragged in the few meetings Shelby had with her about how "The Roach" could get into anything.

Shelby hoped that was true because her current situation was about to test that claim.

The one good thing about visiting Ramona had to do with something the hacker had said the last time she had come up to visit Shelby's family. Ramona claimed to have scrubbed all evidence of her existence from the Mantle, including the broader national data-bases and network. If she'd really accomplished that, Shelby needed her cousin to teach her to do the same thing.

She decided it was better to let Ramona know she was coming. Shelby opened up a closed connection on the car's comm system via the old wireless cell tower network. It was possible this idea wouldn't work, but it was the only way she could think of to remain off the grid and still communicate. If she understood the process and executed it correctly, the conversation would never reach the broader network or the Mantle. The archaic cellular phone network was a relic of the previous century.

The connection rang three times before Ramona picked up, her grainy black and white image hovering over the dashboard. "Geez, Shelby. What are you doing calling me on this old cell network? It doesn't even have a decent video connection."

"I'm in trouble, Ramona. I've got to get somewhere to hide. I think…" Shelby blinked back a fresh surge of tears. "Uh, no, I'm sure Sapiens First killed my parents and are looking for me now, too."

"What? They killed your parents! What are you talking about, Shelby? You're not making any sense."

Shelby wiped at her eyes. She didn't want to go through all this with Ramona right now. "You just have to trust me on this. There were police all around my house. They were bringing the bodies out as I got there. I know it was them, Ramona. I knew I had to get away or I'd be next. I spotted a secret symbol on a sticker. It was on one of the police vehicles. They were with Sapiens First."

"A secret symbol… you have proof that Sapiens First exists?

That's huge, Shelby. Why haven't you published it and gotten the word out? People need to know."

Shelby lost her temper. All the stress finally broke through. "Because the evidence that connects Sapiens First to the symbol comes from that video I released about the Saturday Massacre. If I put it out there now, it'll link the video back to me."

"Shut the front door! You're the one that took the Sapiens rally video that's getting shared everywhere?"

"I didn't record it, but I did spread it to the initial news sites. I was there when it happened and saw the whole thing."

"Oh, my God, you watched and saw Eric murdered right in front of you? Shelby, honey, that's horrible."

"It was awful, Ramona," Shelby muttered through a fresh flow of tears. "There was nothing I could do. All I could do was sit there and watch, knowing what was coming."

"Wait. Back up. You said a second ago that you just left your house and saw Sapiens First people there. How do you know your parents are dead?"

"They have to be. I heard the officer talk about bringing bodies out. You know my mom and dad, Ramona. I can't see them killing anyone. It has to mean they've been killed. I wasn't there when it happened, and managed to get away."

"Are you being followed now?"

"They're not right behind me if that's what you mean, but I have to believe they're looking for me."

"Okay, Shelby I'm cutting off this call right now. Hang up! Don't open this connection again. I know how to get through to you now, but I'll do it through a more secure link. Wait for my call."

As soon as Ramona said that, the call cut off, leaving Shelby sitting in silence, listening to the faint rumble of the pavement under the tires as the automatic navigator drove the car south into the night. Hearing Ramona talk about Eric again brought back all the memories of that horrible day.

Shelby opted not to put on any music. Instead, she sat alone in the darkness of the car's front seat, lit only by the dim lights of the dashboard's control center. Her mind spun through memories of her parents and Eric.

The autonomous vehicle continued south as Shelby broke through the tears once again. It was time to consider her situation. She had food with her if she had to pull over and hide out somewhere.

She was in her parents' car. That was a problem in many ways. She'd already disconnected the car's interface from everything but the Mantle. She couldn't disconnect that unless she wanted to take manual control, which she wasn't all that comfortable doing.

There was also the license plate that could be recognized by automated traffic cameras or other surveillance sources. Hopefully, when Ramona called back, they could figure out an alternative to keep the car on the road and connected to the Mantle without Shelby having to take over behind the wheel. She hated driving.

Shelby sat watching the lights on the highway go by for nearly a half hour before a call finally rang through on the old cell connection again, this time over Shelby's cerebral implant. It surprised her because she wasn't aware her implant even had a chip for that type of signal.

"Hello? Is that you, Ramona?" Shelby said as she opened the anonymous, audio-only call, hoping it was her cousin.

"Shelby, I need you to tell me everything you're doing right now. Is anything around you still connected to the Mantle or any other network?"

"I don't know, Ramona. I think I've disconnected everything I could. I'm no longer hooked in through my implant and I've tried to do everything I can to anonymize my parents' car."

"Wait, you're in your family's car?"

"I had to get away. I'm not a very good driver, Ramona, and I didn't want to disconnect it."

"That's not good. It has to be connected to the Mantle if you're not in manual mode. That causes a huge headache."

"I didn't know what else to do."

"Okay, wait a second while I try something. Is it the same car I saw the last time I was up visiting?"

"Yeah, of course, what else would I be driving?"

"I'm just asking, Shelby. Give me a second. I'm almost done."

Shelby waited for what seemed like forever. All she could hear was a strange clicking sound from the other side of the phone connection. It took her a few seconds before she realized it was the old-style mechanical keyboard Ramona bragged about using all the time. She'd said it kept her connected to the roots of computer hacking from back in the day.

Ramona came back on the line. "All right, I think I got it to work. I'm going to send you something in a burst over this connection to your implant. It's probably going to hurt because this cell connection isn't set up for that kind of bandwidth. It'll also make a God-awful noise that only you are going to be able to hear."

"Okay? I guess I'm ready."

"Here comes."

Whatever Shelby expected based on Ramona's description, she wasn't ready for what happened next. A loud screeching, warbling sound blasted inside her head. It was the audio of raw data being transmitted via an analog audio carrier. Shelby first tried to plug her ears by slapping her hands over the sides of her head. She realized after a few seconds that wasn't going to work since the sound was transmitted directly into her auditory nerve via her implant. A throbbing headache began almost instantly. The pain was so severe that she squeezed her eyes shut and cried out in pain.

"Unnnh, it hurts!"

"Almost done. Hang in there, Shelby."

In the end, she almost blacked out from the pain before the horrible screeching stopped. As the throbbing receded inside her head, Ramona's voice sounded over the connection. "Shelby…, Shelby, are you there? You're not answering me."

"Uh, yes, I'm here. I wasn't prepared for that."

"Yeah, well that was the only way I could get the file to you. Check your implant and see if there's a file there called 'anonymous car.'"

Shelby checked her downloads menu in her implant's database and found it. It was a surprisingly small file considering how long she'd had to endure the pain. The transmission of data using analog audio probably wasn't terribly efficient.

Shelby highlighted the file. "I found it. Now what?"

"I want you to open up a connection to the car's local network port. Don't hook into the car's whole system, just the local port. Once you're hooked in there, you're going to activate the program and direct it to install itself inside the car's firmware system. Got it?"

"Yeah, give me a second while I set it up."

Shelby followed the instructions her cousin gave her and soon had the file installed inside the car's systems.

As soon as the final data check verified the file had transferred, the car swerved to the right, nearly clipping a neighboring vehicle as it careened towards the shoulder. Shelby reached up and grabbed the steering wheel by reflex. She straightened out the car's path just before it hit the guard rail, pulling it back into the far righthand lane on the southbound highway.

Shelby tamped down the terror inside as she struggled to control the vehicle at normal highway speed. She stared straight ahead, holding the steering wheel in a death grip, trying to keep the car inside the lane.

After a few seconds, Shelby said, "Ramona, the car is no longer in auto-mode. It almost drove off the side of the highway before I got control of it."

"Oh, yeah, I forgot to tell you about that. Give it a second. The onboard computer's going to reinstall a new hacked identifier and re-access the wireless system. It'll make the Mantle think it's another car belonging to a retired accountant who lives in Florida. It'll be untraceable back to you."

True to her word, Shelby felt the vehicle take over automatic control again, picking up speed and rejoining the other cars passing by in the automated lanes. She took her hands off the steering wheel.

"Okay, the car is running itself again."

"All right, now you'll have to re-enter the destination into the nav computer. Do it manually using the interface on the dashboard. Don't send it from your implant because I haven't been able to change your implant's identifier yet. I can't figure out a way to do it from here given the narrow bandwidth connection we have. That might have to wait until we get you to my place."

Shelby was glad she didn't have to experience another of those painful burst transmissions. "Do you think you can replace my identifier ID?"

Every implant had a unique identifier serial number that helped the Mantle keep systems connected to the network and organized. The problem was, that also made it easy to search out people and determine their location if you had the right resources. That was why she'd disconnected her own access point once she'd got back in the car near her parents' house.

"I can do it for sure. I haven't done it to anyone other than myself, but I know people who have done it and I've already reached out to them. I'll have the process nailed down by the time you get here. Based on what I can see now through the connection to your vehicle's new identifier, you're about three hours away from my house. Why don't you settle back and get some rest and I'll keep working on my end to come up with some solutions to keeping you off the grid while we figure out what to do next."

"Thanks, Ramona. I don't know what I'd do without you."

"No problem, Shelby. I'm sorry about your parents. They were always pretty decent to me even though I was so weird."

Shelby didn't respond, she just cut the connection. She had thought she'd cried all the tears she had left inside her at her brother's funeral. Now she laid her head back against the headrest, closed her eyes, and let the tears flow as the car drove on into the night.

Shelby didn't realize she'd drifted off to sleep until the car hit a bump in the road that jolted her awake. She checked her internal chronometer. She'd been out for nearly two hours. Shelby realized instantly how worried Cass must be about her since she'd hung up back on the street in front of her parents' house.

She decided to take a risk and use the old cell connection system to reach out to Cass. She wasn't even sure if one of the old towers was still active near Cass's Sapiens enclave but it was worth a try.

The connection rang only once before Cass picked up. "Shelby, is that you?"

"Yeah, it's me."

"Oh my God, I was so worried about you. Why did it take you so long to get back to me? I was certain they'd caught you and had taken you into custody, or worse."

"I'm fine. I had to call my cousin to help me get off the grid. I was driving my parents' car and I knew they'd be able to track me down once they realized it was gone from the house. Then, when Ramona was finished with that, I just sort of fell asleep. I was tired and my head still hurt from the burst download she sent me to hack the car's system."

"I don't know what that means but I'm glad you're all right. Where's your cousin live?"

"Somewhere in the woods in northeastern Pennsylvania. I'm not exactly sure where, but I did have the location in my database so I was able to program the vehicle to drive there. I'm going to stay with her while we figure out what to do next. She's a pretty good hacker and should be able to figure out a way to keep me from being detectable on the grid. I'll stay underground for a while until I figure out what needs to be done next."

"That's probably the best thing to do, Shel. I hope, though, it doesn't mean you can't call me once in a while."

"We'll see. I have to wait and see what Ramona recommends. She's managed to pretty much scrub all evidence of herself off the system, so I'm hoping she can do the same for me."

"What happened when you got out of the car, Shel? What did you find? Why were the police at your house?"

"My parents are dead. Sapiens First got to them while I was out at the store. I guess that means I'm lucky to be alive but I'm angry I wasn't there to help them." Shelby explained what she'd seen at her home before she'd left.

"Shelby, I'm so sorry. You have to know there was nothing you could have done to save them. If you'd been there, they would have killed you or kidnapped you. I think they are closer to catching both of us than ever before. If they're sure you were the one who sent the video, it's only a matter of time until they figure out that I am connected somehow, too. That has to be why Simon Cantwell came to our house today."

"I can't worry about him right now, Cassie. I'm going to go to my cousin's place and I'll be off the grid for a while. I'll call you when I can. I love you."

"I love you, too. Please, please stay safe."

"I'll try the best I can." Shelby cut the connection and closed her eyes again. She was only about an hour away from Ramona's. Her mind drifted back to the last time she'd talked to her mother before she headed to the store. Shelby replayed that conversation over and over again in her head as she drifted back to sleep.

Chapter 15

CASS SAT up in bed after Shelby called. She'd been lying there awake staring at the ceiling worried about why she'd been unable to connect with her girlfriend. Cass had feared the worst until the call finally came through. Now that it was finished, and she knew Shelby was safe and had a plan to stay that way, Cass felt a lot better.

Realizing she wasn't going to be able to fall asleep right now, Cass got up and headed down the hallway to use the bathroom. Maybe she could fall back to sleep afterward.

The house was quiet. It was late and everyone was already asleep in their rooms. At least, Cass thought they were.

As she passed Elena's room, she noticed the door was ajar. She stopped and peeked inside. Elena's empty bed looked like it hadn't been slept in at all.

Cass stepped back out into the hallway and accessed her auditory implant, dialing up the sensitivity to listen for sounds of anyone moving around the house. She picked up the sounds of her father snoring in her parents' room. That was normal.

There were no sounds of anything else out of the ordinary, though. No one was up but herself that she could hear. Either Elena wasn't in the house or she was quieter than usual.

Where had she gone?

Cass turned and headed for the stairs. Maybe she was outside in the driveway getting something out of the car for some reason.

To be sure the kid hadn't fallen asleep on the couch downstairs, Cass did a quick search of the first floor. Elena wasn't there, either. Nor was she in the driveway or anywhere in the back yard.

Cass came back inside and was just about to go and recheck Elena's room, when she noticed something through the front window of the living room. There was a car parked on the street in front of their house. Its lights were out, but the engine was running. Cass dialed in her night vision to try and see who was in the vehicle. The tinted windows defeated even the excellent vision via her implant.

Shaking her head and suspicious of what was going on, Cass headed out the kitchen door into the driveway. From there she could see the rear of the vehicle. There were several years of Enclave High School parking stickers plastered to the back window.

Cass scanned the license plate to check it against public databases but then remembered she couldn't access anything outside the enclave right now.

"Damn, this better not be what I think it is," Cass cursed under her breath.

The parking sticker gave her an idea of what was going on. If her suspicions were correct, Cass was more than slightly annoyed with her little sister.

Her thoughts were confirmed when Cass overheard her sister's voice from inside the vehicle. The enhanced auditory sensor system from her implant picked up the snippet of conversation without any problem at all. It was definitely Elena along with the voice of some boy Cass didn't recognize in the car.

"Phil, stop. I think it's time for me to go inside."

"You don't want me to stop. Why else would you ask me to come over here and park out front this time of night?"

"I just wanted to see you."

"Well, here I am. Come on, let's fool around just a little bit more."

"Um, I guess so. But just for a little while. I have to get inside before anyone figures out I left."

With that, the voices fell silent again.

Cass clenched her fists and marched across the yard to the rear of the sedan, yanking the door open. Inside the backseat was her little sister and Phil Turner, one of the current seniors at Cass's former high school. She recognized him right away. She'd always thought he was a pompous jerk. Seeing him half undressed with his shirt off, tangled up with her sister in the back of his car didn't change her opinion of him.

"Elena, get out of the car."

"Cass, what are you doing here?"

"We'll talk about that when we get in the house. Get out of the car. Don't forget to grab your sweatshirt off the floor before you do. For goodness sake, Elena, what are you thinking? You're only fourteen."

Elena grumbled something Cass couldn't make out, muttered an apology to Phil, and climbed out of the car. Cass could see her sister was embarrassed. By her stance beside the car after she pulled on the sweatshirt over her bra, Elena was also angry. She stood with her arms crossed, glaring at Cass.

Phil sat up and pulled his T-shirt on. He smiled up at Cass. "Hey, Cass. I guess I finally got to fool around with at least one of the Armstrong girls."

Cass shook her fist at the boy smiling up at her from his car. "You pig, if you think you're going to do any more fooling around with Armstrong girls, you've got another thing coming. Wait until I tell my father."

Elena grabbed her arm. "Cassie, you can't tell Dad. He'll be super pissed."

"Fine, I won't tell Dad. You will. If you want to be the grown-up kid at home, then you need to start acting like it. Go up to the house. Phil here is going home."

Phil got out of the back seat and shut the door, then climbed into the front of his car. Before he closed the door, he glanced back at Elena. "I can't believe I wasted my time with a little kid like you. I thought you were grown up enough to know what I wanted from a girl. I guess you're just too young."

Cass reached over and slammed the door shut before he could say anything else hurtful to her sister. The car sped off down the street and disappeared around the corner. Cass turned to Elena, still standing behind her. Tears of embarrassment streamed down the younger girl's cheeks.

"Elena, we need to go back to the house. Come on." Cass reached out to put her arm around her sister's shoulders. Elena shrugged it off and marched up the driveway towards the kitchen door.

Cass sighed and followed behind her. She wasn't sure how she was going to handle this. Elena clearly had done this before. Cass should've figured it out when she first came home based on the way her sister talked about boys.

When they reached the house, Elena marched through the kitchen door and headed straight across the room towards the hallway. Cass reached out and grabbed her arm, yanking her backward, forcing her to turn and face her big sister.

"Don't you just disappear back to your room, Elena. We have to talk about this. Do you understand that he only wanted one thing from you? He was going to use you and then go find some other girl once he was done getting what he wanted."

"I know about boys, Cass, unlike you."

"Just because I'm a lesbian doesn't mean I don't know what boys want. Believe me, I've had to fend off more than my share. Phil was one of them. You heard him. He clearly had an axe to grind when it came to me."

"Oh, so he was only fooling around with me because he wanted to get back at you? I guess I'm still nothing but your little sister, right?" Cass winced as Elena's voice increased in volume.

"Shush! If you keep talking like that, you're going to wake everyone in the house. Unless you want Mom, Dad, and Mr. Cantwell coming down here to see you fully dressed in the middle of the night, with your hair all messed up after rolling around in the backseat of a random boy's car."

Elena reached up and brushed at a strand of hair hanging down beside her face. "You don't understand, Cass. People think differently about me now that you're not around all the time. That's especially true since everybody found out about your new girlfriend. People like me now. They like me just because I'm me. I guess that's going to be different, though, now that you're back again for good."

"I'm not gonna be here for long, Elena. I plan on going back to school, no matter what Mom and Dad want me to do."

"I can't wait until you do. Once you go back, I won't have to worry about you getting in my business and messing up my social life."

"You messed up your own social life, kid."

"Don't call me a kid. I'm old enough to take care of myself."

"Clearly, you're not. If you were, you wouldn't be hiding what you're doing or sneaking out of the house to meet up with some boy in the middle of the night in a car parked in front of our house. Mom and Dad are pretty accepting of a lot of things. They aren't going to be accepting of this."

"So, you are going to tell on me?"

"I want you to tell them. I don't care how you do it, but you need to do it soon. It's important that you own up to this, Elena. If you don't, I will tell them. I'm not going to let you get hurt after I leave, no matter what."

Elena muttered something under her breath that even Cass's superior hearing couldn't make out. Then her sister turned around and left the kitchen, heading upstairs.

Cass let her go this time, realizing they weren't going to get anything worked out here in the middle of the night like this. She shook her head and returned to her room, too. She wasn't sure how she was going to handle what had just happened. Elena needed to know that what she had been doing was wrong. The only thing Cass could think of was to tell her parents about it. If she wasn't going to be around all the time to watch over her sister, they needed to know what she was up to.

There was the problem of what might happen if she told on Elena, though. She had trusted her with a lot since she got home, including her biggest secret of all. Cass was pretty sure Elena wouldn't say anything about her implants, no matter what she did, but not a hundred percent sure. She hated being put in this position by her sister.

Back in her room, Cass climbed into bed and found herself once again wide awake, staring at the ceiling. She worked through her options with Elena and decided to keep an eye on what her sister was up to for a few days before saying anything. Maybe this whole confrontation tonight had scared her into staying out of trouble. It was worth a try before taking any drastic measures.

Cass had an idea and opened up her implant's wireless systems again. She couldn't access the Mantle or any external network, but the dumb internal network inside the Sapiens Movement compound that everyone used was still open to her. Using her implant's superior computing power, it was an easy task of hacking her sister's phone and tablet remotely so she could detect any outgoing or incoming calls.

The tiny subroutine she placed in both devices would notify Cass both when and who Elena talked to. If her sister reached out to Phil, or anybody else like him, Cass would know about it and deal with it appropriately when it happened. In the meantime, she'd have to let things go as they were and hope her sister had learned her lesson now that she'd been caught.

Cass rolled over and pulled the covers up, trying to fall asleep. She finally felt drowsy enough to make a serious attempt at getting some rest. As she drifted off, her thoughts switched between her sister and her worries about Shelby. Even with everything bothering her, Cass's exhaustion from the long hectic day and evening caught up with her and she soon fell asleep.

Chapter 16

WHEN CASS WOKE up the next morning, her feelings had softened about what to do regarding Elena. She figured she'd give her little sister a break this time in hopes that she'd keep herself out of trouble while Cass was home. Hopefully, that would be enough to do the trick.

When Cass went downstairs to get breakfast, her mother and sister were already up in the kitchen cooking.

"Hi, Cassie, your sister and I are just getting something together for breakfast."

"Why don't we all just get what we want as usual?" Cass asked.

"Because Mr. Cantwell is here and we want to show him the best face of our family. Besides, it would be nice to have a real, cooked breakfast together more often. Isn't this better than random bowls of cereal and the like? You know what they say…"

Cass and Elena both rolled their eyes at their mother's favorite breakfast saying. They finished it aloud in unison. "…It's the most important meal of the day."

If there was one thing that Cass's mother was, she was a morning person. She'd been putting up with it her entire life. Her mother's cheerful morning routine was fun for eight-year-old Cassie. It had gotten old quickly by the time she was a teenager.

Sighing because she knew she couldn't win this particular battle, Cass asked, "What do you want me to do?"

"Why don't you go over and start the coffee. Simon and your father are in his office talking about something that came up overnight. It sounded urgent for being so early in the morning. I think they'll be out soon, though. Let's make sure breakfast is ready when they are finished."

Cass headed over to the coffee maker. It was an automated unit so all she had to do was put a pre-filled coffee canister in the receptacle, set it for multiple servings, and make sure the coffee pot was underneath when she pushed the button. It would take a few minutes to fill up the whole insulated container, but when it was done everyone who wanted coffee could have some. Cass went to the cabinet and got out four coffee mugs for herself and the three other adults.

Her mother glanced over her shoulder from where she stood in front of the stove cooking bacon and eggs. "Why'd you get out four mugs, hon?"

Cass didn't understand the question. "Well, there's you, Dad, plus Mr. Cantwell, and me, right?"

Her mom chuckled and went back to tending the food in the frying pan. "I'm not sure I'm going to be able to get used to you like this, Cassie. My big girl, all grown up and drinking coffee just like the rest of us caffeine addicts."

Cass laughed. "Hey, Mom, you know it could be worse."

Elena shot Cass a look from behind her mother's back and tapped the side of her face in the same spot where Cass's implant was.

Cass glared at her. Was she going to say something to their mom in revenge for last night's encounter?

Elena's face broke into a smile and Cass let out a sigh of relief. Her little sister was just messing with her. It wasn't funny, though. Something like that would ruin the whole family.

The coffee finished brewing just as Cass heard her dad and Simon Cantwell come out of the office and into the hallway by the dining room. Cass dialed up her auditory implant to listen to the two men over the clatter of pans and dishes in the kitchen. She wanted to know what the urgent meeting was about.

Her dad said, "I'm sorry you feel like you have to leave so suddenly, Simon. I was looking forward to having you share an office with me for a few days. I thought we could catch up on some things we've meant to get done."

"I'm sorry, James. The update I got from my people in Boston overnight needs my immediate attention."

"I understand. Your work is of supreme importance to the movement right now. I hope you figure out how to track down the person responsible for that video. If this helps you do that, then that's more important than having a few days of rest here at our house. I will make sure you take a rain check, though."

"Fair enough, James. And you're right, there are few things as important as tracking down that sub who's been spreading the lies about us."

"Are you sure you can find out where she is?"

"It shouldn't take us too long. There can't be that many places someone like her can hide out without any extra resources behind her."

Cass stiffened. There could only be one person they were talking about. Simon was leaving to go after Shelby.

The two men came into the kitchen. Cass's father smiled as he entered. "It smells delicious in here. What's the special occasion?"

"I asked the same thing, Dad," Cass said, trying to act normal while her mind spun through ways to stop Simon from leaving.

Her mom laughed as she filled a platter with sausage, bacon, and eggs. "So, sue me for deciding you both needed a nice breakfast this morning. You gentlemen go in and sit down at the dining room table. We'll bring in the stuff we have here. Cassie's got the coffee ready to go."

"Why don't I help you bring some things to the table, Faye,"

Simon offered. "I'll help Cass with the coffee." Cass stiffened for a moment then forced herself to relax as Simon walked towards her. She knew without a doubt her father and Simon were talking about hunting down Shelby. Everything fit together too neatly for it to be anything else.

Forcing a smile on her face, Cass turned towards their guest. "Here you go, Mr. Cantwell. You take these two mugs and I'll bring the other two and the coffee pot."

"Good enough." Simon smiled and took the two mugs from Cass then headed into the dining room behind her father. Cass grabbed the other two cups in one hand and the coffee pot in the other.

When she reached the dining room, she set the mugs down and filled them for her mother and herself before walking around and filling the two cups in front of her father and Simon. The cream and sugar were already on the table and the two men started to make their coffee. Cass set the pot down on a trivet and then sat in her usual seat. She reached for the sugar bowl and the small pitcher of cream and started making her own coffee.

"Goodness gracious, Cassie, that's quite a bit of sugar you're putting in there."

Cass let out a nervous laugh and shrugged. "It's how I like it, Dad. I had to start drinking it when I was staying up late studying at school and the only way I could choke it down in the beginning was with plenty of sugar and cream."

Simon laughed. "You know that's funny, James. I was the same way when I was in the army. I prefer it black now, but back then, I used to have my coffee that same way. I called it blonde mocha." Simon raised his mug in salute to Cass. "To those of us who like our coffee, however we like it."

Cass gave him a half smile and lifted her own mug in his direction before taking a sip. She hated the way he pretended to be friendly when she knew what he was really up to.

Elena and her mother came in with two platters. Cass's mom had filled one with bacon and sausage and put scrambled eggs and toast on the other. They set the two serving plates down in the middle of the table and took their seats.

Cass noticed Elena brought in a mug for herself. She watched as her little sister poured some coffee in it. Everyone at the table stopped talking and watched her as she picked up the mug and took a sip.

When the fourteen-year-old grimaced and shook her head at the bitterness, everyone laughed.

Elena looked up, her face flushing red from top to bottom. "What? I'm big enough to have coffee if I want, aren't I?"

"Well?" Her mom looked over at her husband.

Her father smiled and nodded. "I guess you might be, but if you're going to drink your coffee, you'll probably like it the way your sister does, with plenty of cream and sugar. Why don't you help her, Cass?"

Cass slid the sugar bowl and pitcher of cream over to her sister. "Put the cream in first then add the sugar and stir it up. You can keep adding sugar 'til it tastes right to you, though don't be surprised if it never quite gets there."

Elena smiled and started concocting her version of cafe latte. She still made a little bit of a face when she was finished and took another tentative sip, but she looked up at everyone and smiled at the adults, very pleased with herself.

Cass smiled, too. She knew what Elena was trying to do and it was for Cass's benefit as much as it was for her parents. Elena was telling her big sister she was old enough to make her own decisions in life, including those about boys.

She decided to let things slide for now. Cass wanted to talk more with Elena about what had happened the night before, but now wasn't the time.

Her mom looked up from her plate. "I'm sorry to hear you have to go, Simon. Are you traveling far?"

He shook his head. "No, just up to Boston."

"That's not too bad," her mom remarked. "It's only an hour or so by plane, right?"

"Yes, just a little over that. We've got a lead on something and

I'm going to track it down no matter what. We've got our best people up there on it already and we think we'll be able to get things resolved within a day or two."

As he made the last statement, Simon looked directly at Cass and met her eyes. There was no doubt in her mind he was talking about Shelby now. He gave her a hint of a smile that sent a shiver down her spine, then went back to eating his breakfast.

Cass wanted to scream at him to leave Shelby alone. She knew that wouldn't solve anything. The only thing she could do was find out if Shelby was all right. The problem was, Shelby had gone dark and the only way she was going to talk to anyone was if Shelby initiated the call herself. Hopefully, she'd reach out soon and Cass could tell her what she knew.

After breakfast, her parents walked Simon out to his car in the driveway while Elena and Cass cleaned up the dishes.

Once they were alone, Cass nudged her sister with her elbow as they stood at the sink. "I've decided not to say anything to Mom and Dad, squirt."

"Really? What changed your mind?"

"I decided that embarrassing you was enough of a punishment. I hope you understand what I was trying to tell you, though. Boys like Phil are nothing but trouble. Find somebody closer to your own age. You'll be much happier in the long run."

"The boys my age are idiots, Cass. Remember when you were fourteen? I know you liked girls and all, but you remember what idiots boys were at that age, right?"

"Honestly, Elena, according to Mom, boys are rarely anything but idiots. Even when they're grown and old enough to make decisions for themselves, they often make bad ones when it comes to girls."

They both laughed at that.

"Seriously, though, I want you to be careful. You can't afford to get yourself into any kind of trouble that you can't get out of. I won't always be here to help you. You know how Mom and Dad will react if they catch you."

"Yeah, but you're gonna be around for a while, right?"

"I can't stay here too long, Elena. You saw what happened with my face. The patch is temporary and will eventually wear out unless I get a new one. Think about it. Where am I going to get that kind of thing around here?"

Elena handed Cass another plate to put in the dishwasher and shook her head. "I don't know, maybe we can take a trip into town just the two of us and find someplace there. I mean, you found a place to get that thing to begin with."

"That was in the city. Small towns around here aren't going to have anything like what I need. And even if they did, most likely someone there will recognize me or word of it will get back to people here in the enclave. Small towns are like that, even with people like us. Someone's bound to say something."

"You know Mom and Dad don't want you going back. How are you going to get around that?"

"I told them, just like I told you. I am still going back, no matter what. I'll figure out a way to make it work. I don't know how yet, but I will."

Elena fell silent and the two of them finished up the dishes without saying anything else. They didn't get a chance to talk anymore because their parents returned from seeing Simon off.

Her mom smiled as she entered the kitchen. "Oh, good, you cleaned everything up for me. I was just telling your father how grown-up you two have gotten. You girls are drinking coffee and all and now this. It makes me think that you two can take care of your-selves well enough that maybe your father and I can finally go on a vacation, just the two of us."

"I like the sound of that," Her father said. He reached out and pulled his wife close, leaning down and giving her a kiss. Her mom leaned into the kiss and reached around her husband to pull him closer into the embrace.

Elena mimed sticking her finger down her throat. "Ewww! Seri-ously, Mom and Dad, stop it."

Cass nodded. "Yeah, Elena's right. I can't even begin to wipe that image out of my head."

Cass's mom and dad both laughed as they separated.

"Your father and I have always been close, girls. There's no reason for you two to be embarrassed when we show affection to each other."

Elena rolled her eyes. "There's affection, Mom, and then there are disgusting displays of stuff like that."

Her dad laughed. "Well, perhaps I should take your mother to our bedroom then."

All three women in the kitchen shouted at the same time. Her mom laughed as she shook a finger at him then reached over and swatted her husband playfully on the rear end as he hurried from the kitchen, laughing the whole way to his office.

"Seriously, Mom," Cass said. "That's just gross."

"You don't hear me complaining about you and your friends…" Her mom stopped talking as soon as she realized she was referring to Shelby at this point in Cass's life. "Never mind. Just remember, I don't complain about you and your love interests."

Her mom turned and left the kitchen, her face filled with a complex mix of emotions Cass couldn't begin to read.

Both Cass and her sister shared a glance.

Elena pursed her lips and shook her head. "That was awkward, Cass. We really have to figure out a way to get them to accept your girlfriend."

"I'm not sure that's ever going to be an option, Elena. Especially now with things the way they are with me." Cass reached up and brushed her cheek with her right hand. She'd been self-conscious about whether the patch was staying sealed in place ever since Elena had seen her face without it.

"Don't worry, Cass. If things start to show or peel away again, I'll make sure you know before Mom and Dad see anything. I just hope you remember that I have your back when you need it the most."

Elena left the room before Cass could respond. She wanted to tell her sister that helping to hide a medically necessary cyber implant was different than covering up for irresponsible behavior with boys who were way too old for a fourteen-year-old girl.

Cass shook her head. She worried this was all going to come to a head at some point and she was going to have to make a difficult decision about what to do about Elena. Cass dried her hands and dropped the towel on the counter. It was time to head up to her room. She wanted to try and see if she could get through the firewall somehow.

Chapter 17

AS CASS SHUT her bedroom door and lay down on her bed, the rest of the house moved on with their normal activities for the day. She could hear her mother vacuuming somewhere in the house as the machine's hum drifted up to her.

Cass's father had returned to his office with the door closed. She wasn't sure where Elena was. She was probably in her room listening to music. Now was the perfect time for Cass to try and get through the firewall again. She needed to do that if she was going to be able to reach out to Shelby.

Shelby had been able to contact her over one of the old closed cell connections, but that was from an anonymous number. Cass couldn't return that call so she had to make sure she was ready for any further communication that might come in from her girlfriend.

The cell phone call the night before had surprised Cass. She didn't know her implant carried a chip that accessed that system, given how outdated it was. Nobody used the old cell towers anymore and there'd been talk of tearing them down in most parts of the country. They stayed up and transmitting because there were still some old framework business systems that operated on those carriers.

Cass closed her eyes as she checked the *protocol one* program in her implant. It was still rimmed in a pulsing red glow. She wasn't sure what that meant, but it had been that way since the firewall incident the day before. Cass decided to run the program anyway because Derek had assured her it was intuitive and should be able to learn what it needed to spoof the firewall and other security systems.

She opened the folder and ran the system check before engaging the *protocol one* program and watching it push out from her mind into the surrounding wireless network to do its work.

As soon as the program engaged with the network, a shooting pain lanced through her mind. Without knowing it, Cass cried out at the sudden attack on her implant. Squinting through the pain, she immediately shut down all wireless access. It was almost too late.

Cass woke up a few seconds later. She found herself laying back in her bed with her eyes squeezed shut and her hands pressed into her temples. Cass rubbed the side of her face and tried to stop the pounding, throbbing pain in her head.

"What the hell was that?" she said aloud to herself.

Cass checked her systems and ran a basic diagnostic on her implant, searching for any permanent damage. The *protocol one* file was now grayed out. She couldn't access it or open the folder at all now. It was as if it didn't exist anymore or had been deleted from her system somehow.

Cass wasn't sure what that meant, but it couldn't be good. Without that program to rely on, Cass had no access to the outside world beyond what she could get from Elena and her connection to her friend, Cadence.

Cass left her room to head down to Elena's room. As she approached Elena's door, the doorbell rang. Cass didn't hear anyone heading to the door to answer it, so she headed down the stairs to get it herself.

Before she got there, the doorbell rang again, twice this time, close together as if there was a sense of urgency behind it. She opened the door to see Cadence's father, Mr. Benson, standing there. He had a massive grin on his face.

"Hi, Cass. I was hoping to see if your father was here. I have some news he'll be pleased to hear."

"Sure, come on in. He's in his office, but I'll get him."

"That's great. I'll wait here."

Cass started down the hallway but stopped because her father came around the corner in her direction. "Who's at the door, Cassie?"

"It's Mr. Benson, Dad. He seems excited about something."

"Well, let's see what he wants."

Cass followed her Dad back to the front door. She planned on tagging along to listen in if she could. Mr. Benson's arrival right after her catastrophic run-in with the enclave's network worried her.

Her dad shook Aaron Benson's hand. "What's going on, Aaron? You seem excited about something."

A huge grin spread across the other man's face. "I got him, James. The bastard tried to hack the system again just a few minutes ago. I'd set up a little trap for them after the last time and they fell for it. Whatever program they were using to hack us is toast. They should've used a different one because this time I tracked it back to them."

"Really? That's great news. So, who is it?"

"Well, I'm not exactly sure. But here's the news. It's not someone outside the enclave. Whoever it is, they're already inside the walls. On top of that, I got an excellent read on their equipment. They're not using a tablet or laptop computer, James. My system picked up the unmistakable signature of a medical grade cybernetic implant."

It was clear from the look on Cass's father's face that Aaron Benson had his full attention right now. "I thought our system was supposed to keep people like that out, Aaron. That's your job isn't it?"

Mr. Benson's shoulders sagged a little at the rebuke. "Yeah, I'm sorry. You're right, of course." The IT specialist seemed only a bit cowed by the admission. He continued right away, saying, "There is one thing in our favor, Mr. Armstrong. I'm pretty certain I fried their implant. The system I put in place was set up to overload any network device that tried using that other foreign program to hack us again. It was set up to send a massive burst of data traffic over the return connection. It should have pretty much shut down any system that was running it. I figure all we have to do is send security around the enclave and check on everyone. All we have to do is look for a person lying catatonic on the ground. Believe me, they're not getting up and walking around after what I did to them."

"I guess I should commend you then, Aaron. That sounds like you've done good work. Why don't you go ahead and call out the security team on my say-so? Get them started on a house by house sweep."

Aaron snapped his shoulders back and started to salute but stopped himself. He smiled and nodded instead. "Got it. I'll report back when we're finished. Hopefully, we find the bastard."

"When you find the person you're looking for, bring them to me. I want to find out who this interloper is."

Her dad shut the door as Mr. Benson left and turned back to Cass. "See what these people are capable of, Cassie? They know they're not welcome here and yet they break in anyway. That's what you have to watch out for. The Mantle is subverting anyone connected to it. Eventually, subs won't be able to control themselves and they'll just do the Mantle's bidding all the time. That's what we're fighting against."

Cass wanted to say something but didn't want to get in a fight with him right now. Part of it was because of the massive headache she still had. She also needed to go back up to her room and check on some things. She was worried Mr. Benson was right about what he'd done, even if she wasn't catatonic on her bedroom floor right now. Maybe that data burst had damaged her implant in some way. She needed to run a full system check and diagnostic analysis.

"Dad, I don't want to have this talk with you right now. I'm going up to my room. I hope you find whoever it is you're looking for."

"We will, Cassie. There's nowhere they can hide in here. Aaron is very good at what he does. He'll track them down eventually."

That was what Cass was afraid of. She started up the stairs as her father returned to his office.

Cass thought about what might happen if they didn't find the person they were looking for. It only meant Mr. Benson was going to try something else. Cass again wished she could call out through the firewall. She needed to contact Derek and see if there was anything he could do to restore the *protocol one* file. She would inevitably be discovered without it. There was no way she could turn off her implant entirely because of the medical nature of it. If she did, it would make her comatose and unable to function.

Cass decided she needed to talk to Elena. Maybe her sister could get Cadence to help out somehow. She didn't want to tell Cadence everything, but maybe Cass could finagle a little lie to get another password or some other way to call out from the younger girl.

Cass tapped on Elena's door.

"Yes?"

Cass opened it. "Hey, can I come in?"

"Sure. What's up?"

Cass nodded and stepped inside, closing the door behind her. Elena sat on the floor playing a game or something on her tablet. She took off her headphones. Cass could hear the music playing over the tiny speakers in the earpieces.

"Elena, I wondered if you could get in touch with your friend Cadence again. I've got a problem."

"What is it?"

"Cadence's father set some kind of trap for me on the enclave's network. When I opened up to the network a little while ago, something happened and it erased or broke down my hacking program. It's like I'm blind to the outside world now. I was hoping maybe Cadence would have a way around it."

"Cass, Cadence is cool and everything, but she'll never be all right if we tell her about you having that implant. She'll tell her father right away."

"Well, maybe we don't tell her it's the implant. Maybe we tell her I have some other sort of connected device from college and I want to talk to my girlfriend. Isn't that what you told her before?"

"It is." Elena paused for a second and nodded. "That might work. Cadence is super bright in some ways, but not so much in others. I think she might enjoy chatting with us about why you need it, though. She's a hopeless romantic and reads all sorts of stories like that. She knows about Shelby and she still gave us the password before, so clearly, she's rooting for you two. Maybe we can use that to get some more access passwords or something out of her."

"That's what I was hoping you'd say. When do you think we can get over to see her?"

"Let me reach out to her. I'll send her a text message and see if she's available to catch up this morning. Her dad works over at the security office and her mom has a job in town. She's home all by herself during the day when we're not at school. Maybe we can go over there for lunch. I'll see if we can order something from delivery and we can meet at the gate and then take it over to her place."

"Sounds like a good plan. I'll even pay for it."

"Of course, you will. I'm not paying for this. I don't have that much money anyway."

Cass smiled. She still had money left over from what her parents sent for her vacation to the islands. She never spent all of it because she spent most of the time in the hospital which was covered by her school health insurance.

After a quick exchange of text messages, the lunch arrangements were made. Cadence seemed excited to have them both come over.

When lunchtime arrived, they used Elena's tablet to reach out to a sub shop in town and order a pizza, some chicken wings, and some cheesecake for dessert. The delivery places around the enclave sent automated robots out once the food was ready. They weren't allowed to come into the enclave, but people ordered from them anyway and picked up the food at the front gate.

After they ordered, Elena and Cass set out for the compound's main entrance. The chilly winter air was almost mitigated by the midday sun as they walked through the enclave.

The automated delivery bike showed up a few minutes after they got to the front gate. It sat idling just outside, waiting for them.

Elena started forward alone to retrieve the food and then stopped and looked back at Cass. "Aren't you coming to help me?"

"I can't go out there. If I cross through the perimeter firewall again, the system will alert Mr. Benson. He'll take one look at the security cameras and they'll know it's me for sure."

Elena nodded and went outside the enclave using a small, manually operated pedestrian gate situated next to the main one for vehicular traffic. She slipped Cass's credit chip into the reader on the robot delivery vehicle. It was a motorized, three-wheeled tricycle of sorts with a large metal box mounted over the two rear wheels above the motor.

As the delivery bot popped the chip back out to Elena, one of the doors on the side of the box popped open revealing several brown paper bags and a cardboard pizza box inside. Elena slid the box of pizza out, balancing the two bags on top and shut the door. As soon as she closed it, the automated trike sped away.

Elena came back through the gate and handed the pizza box with the bags on top of it to Cass. "Here you go. I figured since I went out and got it, you can carry it."

"Fair enough."

Cass and Elena headed back through the enclave's neighborhoods towards the Benson home. Cass hoped this potential solution worked out or she was as good as caught.

Chapter 18

THE TWO OF them headed through the enclave on foot until they got to Cadence's street. Just as Elena had said, the driveway was empty and there was no garage. The Benson's two cars were not there and that would give the three girls some privacy as they chatted over lunch.

Cass and Elena walked over to the side of the house and rapped on the kitchen door. Cass saw Cadence through the door's window. She ran over to them, her face beaming with a big grin.

"Hey ladies, it's great to see you. I'm so happy you two decided to come over. I was surprised when you called."

Cadence was short and a little overweight. Her face had a bit of an acne problem, even though such things were typically easy to manage with a little bit of medication nowadays. It might mean her parents were super strict with regards to what kind of technologies they made available for their daughter. Some Sapiens Movement parents had rules that were more stringent than others and considered any type of the new gene manipulation medications off-limits, just like artificial intelligence was for the rest of the community.

Cass smiled as she entered the Benson's home. "I'm glad you let us come over, Cadence. We need some help with something and figured maybe we could come over and have lunch and chat about it."

"Absolutely. I'm so excited you're here. Come on in."

They followed Cadence into the kitchen with Elena leading the way. The home was a small rancher about half the size of the Armstrong's two-story house.

Cass set the pizza box and bags down on the kitchen counter. She looked around. "Cadence, do you have plates or something we can eat on?"

"We have paper plates. They're in that cabinet just in front of you."

Cass smiled. "Great, why don't you two get us something to drink. Then we can sit down and chat while we eat."

Elena and Cadence went to the fridge and pulled out three bottles of soda. Cass found the paper plates and grabbed three of them before bringing them over to a raised portion of the kitchen counter. There were barstools set around it which allowed the three of them to sit and eat right there in the kitchen.

Cadence popped open the pizza box and slid out a slice of the pepperoni pizza inside. "Mmmm, I love Pizza Boy pizza."

"Me too," Cass said. "Even in the big city, they don't make pizza like this. Pizza Boy knows how to make pizza better than anyone else I've found."

Cadence grinned as she finished her first bite. "That's funny, Cassie. I figured the city would have good pizza, too. You know, it's kind of cool how you went and lived there like that this year. You must've seen a lot of cool stuff."

Cass shrugged. "It was pretty awesome in a lot of ways. Things are a lot different than we think they are outside of the enclave."

"Oh, I know. Ever since I was little, I've been looking over my dad's shoulder while he worked. I learned early on how to hack out of the enclave's systems. I've been doing it for a long time. I was able to get into the mass market entertainment networks by the time I was eight without anyone noticing it. I know all about what goes on outside."

"Really?" Cass said. Her estimation of what Cadence could do increased a little bit after hearing that. "What else do you know about the outside?"

"Oh, a whole lot of stuff. I've told Elena about some of it. There's a lot of people out there and everyone has something that's connected to the Mantle in their homes. They may not go as far as some do getting personal implants, but everyone's got a refrigerator, or a toaster, or just their home computer all connected. I don't think the Sapiens Movement is going to get people to give up all that stuff no matter what the grownups think will happen. I've begun to think that maybe the Sapiens Movement is a lost cause."

Cass couldn't hide her shock at the bold words coming from the girl. It was enough to get her mandatory re-education in one of the movement's special camps. "That's a bold thing to say, Cadence. For someone your age, it could get you sent away. If it were someone like me, well, they'd chuck me out entirely."

"I'm careful with whom I talk to. I figured with your girlfriend and all, you probably aren't going to turn me in."

Cass smiled and nodded. "You're right. Your secret's safe with me, and Elena, too. Right, squirt?"

Elena waved her hand at Cadence sitting next to her. "Oh, Cadence and I are best buds."

Cadence nodded as she took another huge bite of pizza. As she chewed the food, she smiled and said, "So, what did you both need?"

Elena gestured with her slice of pizza at Cass between bites. "I think it's my sister that needs something."

Cass nodded. "Um, yeah, I was wondering if you could help me connect a device I brought in from outside the enclave. I know I really shouldn't have it, but I didn't want to leave it at school. When I opened it up this morning, it couldn't connect to the outside, and then it just sort of shut down. It caused all kinds of problems I think."

Cadence leaned forward and slapped her hand on the top of the counter. "You're the reason my dad's been running around all morning like a chicken with its head cut off." She started laughing until tears came to her eyes.

"What do you know about that?" Cass asked.

"Only that he thought he caught some sub hiding here in the enclave. He was sure there was some person with some kind of medical implant that had gotten it through the firewall and security wards somehow. I wasn't so sure based on what I saw going across the data stream on his tablet when I stole a look. Now, I'm positive. Did his little security program damage your device at all?"

"No, thank goodness. It messed up some files, but that's it. It's a special tablet I got to use at school. I wanted to use it to talk to Shelby, but I was unable to get through the network when they caught me the first time. I tried to hack my way out this morning and well, you know what happened then."

Cadence giggled. "Yeah. My dad was so excited he went running over to your house right away. It's pretty funny; he was so close to the source of the breach the whole time."

Cass and Elena exchanged a glance. The girl was closer to the truth than she knew, even if she had one key detail figured wrong.

Cass cleared her throat after swallowing a bite of her pizza. "Anyway, Cadence, I was hoping you could help me figure a way to use my device to communicate through the firewall again. Is there some sort of port or something you can open up for me like you did before?"

Cadence shook her head. "It's not going to be that easy this time around. Dad found and closed down a lot of those openings I created over the years. A lot of them were back doors I installed into the system myself. His review of the security wards found most of them. He doesn't know I did it, he just went ahead and shut them down."

Cass's shoulders sagged a little.

Cadence must've noticed. "Have no fear though, Cass. There is a way. Did you bring the tablet with you?"

"No. I didn't want my parents to see it. They would've known what it was right away. I left it in my room."

Cadence paused in thought then announced, "That makes it a little more difficult, but not impossible. Let me think for a few minutes."

Cadence got up from her stool and walked across the kitchen where she picked up a large computer tablet about twelve inches across at its widest point. She set it down on a pop-up stand on the central counter and climbed back onto her stool. She waved her hand, deploying a virtual keyboard over the countertop, and began typing away.

Cass leaned over to look at the screen. All she saw where numbers and letters streaming by. She realized Cadence was accessing and adapting direct computer code.

Cass pointed at the screen. "Wow, that's impressive, Cadence. You're quite the programmer, aren't you?"

"I want to go to MIT someday. I want to be one of their best coders ever."

"MIT?" Cass asked. "That's a big school. It's even more daring than me going down to City University."

"Oh, I'm going whether they let me go or not. I'm not going to wait for permission. I'll just pack up and leave at some point and never come back. I am through with the Sapiens and their backward ways, Cass. I am going to change the world someday with my software."

Elena smiled. "I told you, Cass. Cadence is going places."

"Yes, you did."

Cass leaned back and ate another slice of pizza while Cadence continued working on her tablet. Every minute or so she'd pause long enough to take another bite of pizza, wipe her hands off, and then go back to work on the virtual keypad displayed in front of her.

Elena pulled out her phone and began looking at something while she waited.

Cass kept her attention focused on Cadence. She was putting a lot of trust in this girl. She hoped it paid off.

A half-hour after she started, Cadence smiled and snapped her fingers. "Got it. I was able to reconfigure one of the worms I use to drill through the firewall. I can set up the program now so that it gets installed on any device. It won't be quite as elegant as what I do here manually when I can program on the fly, but it should get any system that's got Mantle access through the firewall and connected again."

Cass raised her eyebrows in surprise. "Any system? I find that hard to believe. You mean that could even get, let's say a medical grade implant, outside the firewall."

Cadence shrugged. "Sure. They all use the same basic software routines to access the Mantle and other wireless systems. They might have other sub-routines running in the background, but everything runs on the same base code nowadays."

Cass didn't know if that was true or not but she had to accept that the girl knew what she was talking about. It was a considerable risk installing anything from outside onto her implant. She'd done it once already with Derek. Now she was trusting a fourteen-year-old girl's computing capabilities with her safety and maybe her life, if it somehow corrupted her implant's basic coding.

Cass decided she was all in at this point. "So, how do I install it?"

Cadence smiled. "I'll give you a chip with a wireless transceiver in it. All you need to do is hold it up next to the device. It should pair with any wireless connection automatically and open up a file on the device's interface. I've named that file ' Cass's Secret.'"

Cadence grinned as she said the name and continued her instructions. "Just run the program, follow the prompts, and you're home free. You'll be talking with Shelby in no time."

"That's awesome, Cadence. I owe you one."

Cadence waved it off with one hand and pointed at Cass's sister. "That's okay. Like she said, we are best buds. You know she's trying to get me hooked up with Donny Glenn. She says he kind of likes me."

Cass shot her sister a glance.

Elena looked up from her phone. "Yeah, I've almost got him convinced that he should take the leap and ask you out for lunch."

Cadence giggled and smiled from ear to ear. Cass was a little embarrassed at deceiving the girl this way. She clearly was on Cass's side even if she didn't know everything about what she'd just done. She was no strict Sapiens member, even if she'd been raised here.

Cass got up from her stool and started cleaning up their trash. They'd finished the pizza and most of the wings. She wrapped the rest of the wings up in foil for Cadence and put them in the refrigerator.

Gathering up the empty bags and the pizza box, Cass turned to Cadence. "Where do you want me to put these?"

"You can put them out in the garage through the back door to the yard. There's a bin out there and they'll go in the recycling with the paper plates and everything else."

Cass went out into the yard and set the pizza box, bags, and other paper goods in the recycling bin there. She turned around and stopped dead in her tracks. There on the wall, hanging from a hook inside the back door, next to some assorted cables and wires, was a large belt pouch like a fanny pack. It had a coiled cord extending from it leading to a long metal tube shoved in a leather sleeve attached to the belt.

A symbol stood out on the black fabric of the fanny pack. It was a clenched white fist inside a white circle which Cass recognized as the symbol of the Sapiens First terrorist movement.

Cass knew that device all too well. It looked identical to the one Simon Cantwell had used to kill Shelby's brother and the other six cyber humans. Had Cadence's father designed the device that fried Eric's brain, killing him?

She didn't know the answer, but given what she was staring at, she felt more than a little foolish for sharing so much with Cadence. Could it have all been an act?

Cass went back into the kitchen. Cadence and Elena chatted about boys, oblivious to the expression on Cass's face. Cass tried to collect herself as she puttered around the kitchen a little bit, straightening up. Then she said, "We should probably get that chip from you and head back home. Mom probably needs our help with something around the house this afternoon, don't you think, Elena?"

Thankfully, Elena took the hint and nodded. "I'll call you later, all right, Cadence?"

"That would be great. You still need to tell me when Donny's going to meet me for lunch."

"I should know any day now."

Elena and Cass headed out to the street. They started walking down the sidewalk through the community towards where the Armstrongs lived. Cass put her hand in her pocket. She had the custom-programmed wireless chip there. She was a little worried about using it now, after what she'd seen in the Benson's home.

What if Cadence was messing with her and came up with a way to fry whatever device came close to that chip? Cass wasn't sure she wanted to take the risk.

"Hey, squirt, what do you think of Cadence. Is she really that reliable or was all of that talk an act?"

"She hates this place, Cass. She literally can't wait to get out of here. I think by the time she's fifteen next year, she will have maxed out on all the science and math programs they can teach here in the enclave. Once that happens, I wouldn't be surprised if she just ran away and headed to Boston to go to MIT all on her own. That's all she talks about when she's alone with me anymore. Well, that and Donny. Why do you ask?"

"I'm a little worried, that's all. I saw something in their garage that leads me to think her father's mixed up with something that might be more dangerous than just being the cybersecurity director here."

"What do you mean?"

"I think he's a member of Sapiens First."

"But Daddy always says that's nothing but a myth."

Cass took a chance and kept talking. "They're not. They're very real and very dangerous. Simon Cantwell is one of them, too. He might even be their leader."

"How could you possibly know that?"

"You remember that tattoo on his arm? He left his sleeves rolled up when we were eating dessert after cleaning up from dinner. You must've seen it."

"Yeah. I saw it. It was pretty cool. I thought maybe he got it in the army or something."

"That's the symbol of Sapiens First. I saw them in that video that went around."

"The fake video? You heard Dad. You can't trust that thing."

"You're wrong. I can trust it. It's real, Elena. Everything in that video really happened. Have you even seen it?"

"No, you know they don't let us see stuff like that here inside the enclave and I never went looking for it when I could peek through the firewall. I hear it's pretty nasty and graphic. Since it's all fake, though, who cares?"

"It's not fake, Elena. I know for sure it isn't. When those people were killed in that video, the person who killed them had the same tattoo in the exact same place as Mr. Cantwell. That's how I know who he is. There's something in the Benson's garage, something horrible, with that same image on it that leads me to believe Mr. Benson is mixed up with it somehow, too."

"I don't know, Cass. It all seems a little far-fetched. I mean, how do you know all that, just from being outside at school for a few months? You talk like you were there at the rally when it all happened."

Cass bit her lip, then decided she'd said so much already, she may as well go all the way. "I wasn't just there, Elena. I recorded the video via my ocular and cerebral implants. I saw the whole thing and I have the whole recording up here to prove it. It was awful. I had it zoomed in to try and find out where Shelby's brother was. I finally found him on stage just before they killed him. While I watched and recorded it, Shelby streamed it out from her tablet."

Cass stopped walking when she realized Elena was no longer next to her. She turned. Her sister stood a few feet behind her, staring at her with her mouth open.

"Come on, Elena. Don't freak out on me. Nothing's changed. It's just I saw something horrible and now I have to live with it. I told you because I trust you more than just about anyone right now."

Elena finally found her words again and shook her head. "Cassie, that must've been horrible. And Shelby's brother was one of the ones who was killed?"

"Yeah, and now I think Mr. Cantwell is chasing after Shelby with other members of their group. That's why he had to leave in a hurry to go to Boston. It's also why I have to reach out to Shelby and make sure she's safe. I got through to her briefly last night and said enough to warn her. Now she's on the run and I'm worried about her."

"Isn't it already too late?"

Cass shook her head. "No, Shelby got away from some people trying to catch her last night and took off to go into hiding. She thinks they killed her parents at her house and now they're after her. She called me before she turned off her access to hide her location. Now I need to reach out to her, but to do that, I have to be able to get through the firewall. That's why we had to go see Cadence."

Elena smiled and walked up next to her sister as the two started walking again.

Cass glanced at Elena while the strolled down the sidewalk together. "What are you grinning about?"

"I'm sure glad you're home, Cass. Nothing this exciting ever happens when you're gone."

"I could do with a little less excitement right now. Let's go back to the house so I can see if the hack Cadence came up with actually works."

Chapter 19

THE INTERNAL ALARM in Shelby's implant sounded and woke her up with a start. It took her several seconds to remember where she was. Sitting up, Shelby rubbed her eyes and tried to get back in sync. She was tired, both physically and mentally, but she remembered she was at her cousin Ramona's house. A check of her internal chronometer showed it was well past noon. She'd been asleep for a long time.

Shelby sat on a ratty, orange plaid sofa from another century in a low-ceilinged basement. The cheap wood paneling on all the walls and the worn, shag carpeting all gave off a look at something out of a period holo-drama from almost a hundred years before.

Across the room, a clothes washer and dryer sat side-by-side in an alcove beneath a simple set of wooden stairs. Shelby shook her head and pressed against her temples with her fingertips, massaging her head with gentle circular motions. Her head still hurt from the data blast Ramona had sent her the night before while she was driving down to Pennsylvania.

Shelby stood up and walked over to the stairs. She heard footsteps above. Someone was up and around in the kitchen. She'd been here once before, a long time ago when she was little, and she remembered playing with Ramona in this basement. This was Shelby's cousin's childhood home.

Ramona was an only child, born late in her parents' lives. When her parents had passed away a few years back, Ramona had told the whole family she'd sold the house at auction to someone else. Of course, that was all part of her plan.

Only recently had Shelby discovered that Ramona had repurchased the home from herself using a false identity. That was one of the reasons Shelby decided this was the place for her to come and try and disappear. Ramona Roche was as close to being untraceable as Shelby thought someone could be.

As Shelby started to ascend the stairs, Ramona, a tall and gangly red-head, stepped into the doorway at the top of the steps. "Oh, I was just getting ready to call down to you. You said you wanted to get up about now. I know it's after lunchtime, but I usually eat breakfast about now. I have some toaster waffles if you want to something to eat."

Ramona turned and disappeared back into the kitchen as Shelby climbed the stairs behind her.

"Ramona, I wanted to thank you again for having me. I didn't know where else to go."

Ramona flashed Shelby a toothy grin. "Believe me, this is great. I've been looking for a way to stick it to the Sapiens First bastards for years."

"Yeah, but everybody thought you were just spouting off when you talked about them at the last family reunion. I never really believed in them either, until I saw what they did to Eric."

Ramona tapped the right side of the implant that circled the back of her head. "Yeah, well, you wouldn't believe the amount of data I have stored up here about them, and a lot of other things, too."

Shelby sat down at the kitchen table and reached up to run her fingers through her hair, as she still struggled to wake up. "Have you had any luck figuring out how to get me to disappear?"

"I've got a few ideas. It's going to be tricky, because you've already shown up on the tracking systems. Someone is definitely looking for you. Usually, when you eradicate a person, it helps for them to be off the radar to begin with. Then no one notices when little bits of the database change here and there. Don't worry, though. I'm on it. We'll get it done."

"I hope so. I still can't figure out how this all happened. I didn't think they'd be able to find me."

Ramona walked over and sat down in the chair next to Shelby. She laid a hand on her cousin's arm and gave it a squeeze of reassurance. "How sure are you about what happened to your parents?"

"I heard one of the police officers say they were bringing two bodies out. My parents were the only ones home, so it's got to be them."

"I did a search of police records in the Boston area, and there are no reports of any fatalities with your parents' names associated with them. They may not be in the system yet or are still being seen by the coroners, but I'll keep an eye out for them. Is it possible something else happened and you misunderstood?"

Shelby tamped down her anger as emotions started to rise to the surface. "I didn't misunderstand. The only other option is that my two older parents somehow took out two people from a Sapiens First hit squad and then called the police. Somehow, I doubt that's the case."

Ramona shrugged. "I'm only telling you to keep an open mind. They might just be screwing with you. Stranger things have happened in this world."

"It doesn't matter now. Even if they're still alive somehow, I can't go back. It would be too dangerous for them. We have to figure out how the Sapiens team found me and keep it from happening again."

The electric toaster popped up the first round of frozen waffles. Ramona crossed the kitchen and grabbed two plates, putting a waffle on each of them and returning to the table.

She handed one to Shelby. "The Sapiens First hackers are pretty damn good considering their stance on technology. At this point, they probably know everything there is to know about that video you put out on the net."

"I tried to anonymize it, but I guess I didn't do a good enough job. Maybe if I'd…"

Ramona playfully poked Shelby in the shoulder with two fingers. "Stop that. Blaming yourself isn't going to solve anything. Those monsters killed your parents, not you. You shouldn't have to hide from anyone for showing the truth to the world."

"I know, but…"

Ramona shook her head. "No buts about it. Now, eat your waffle. I'll put another one down for each of us."

Ramona went over to the freezer and pulled out a package with two more waffles in it, popping them in the toaster's slots and dropping them down to heat. Shelby started digging into her waffle. She didn't really like things that were too sweet, so she opted not to add syrup to it.

The batter they used to make the waffle had some sugar in it, so it was sweet enough for her already. As she chewed her first bite, Shelby thought about Cass. If they'd found her, could they trace it back to Cassie somehow, as well? Shelby asked Ramona the question.

Ramona sat down and slathered butter all over her waffle before drowning it in syrup. "Hmmm, it's possible they traced it back to her. I really need to figure out how they identified you first and take a look at the original video for myself. If I can uncover hidden stuff about it, they can discover the same things, too."

"I'm worried about Cass. She's trapped in that enclave already and she's having trouble getting through the firewall to communicate with me."

"I can't imagine what it must've been like for her growing up in there. I know you say she's a really decent person, but I wonder how she lived all those years with monsters like that and isn't twisted herself in some way."

A hint of ire filled Shelby's voice as she jumped to defend her girlfriend. "She's not a monster at all, and from what I can tell, her sister isn't, either. I think they're all simply people who've been misguided by someone who told them things that made them afraid."

"That doesn't excuse the horrible things their terrorist arm does on their behalf."

"Of course, it doesn't. I'm only saying that most of the people are probably pretty decent, and just fearful of technology because of what unscrupulous people have told them. I suspect the true believers are limited in number."

Ramona added yet more butter to the remainder of her waffle and then drowned it in even more syrup. She set the syrup back down and shoveled a huge piece into her mouth.

Shelby shook her head and smiled. Ramona had always been a little bit strange. She was also the best person to help Shelby right now, and maybe Cass, too.

Shelby ate some more of her waffle and sat back in her chair. "Once we're done with breakfast, what's the plan?"

"I want you to download the video to my system in the other room. Then I'll start analyzing it, while I run a sweeper program to find any trace of your whereabouts and erase it. We've got a lot to get done to make sure no one knows where you are. Then we can get started changing your identity to something new."

"Do you think they might have followed me here?"

"I watched your scrambled signal all the way in. Between my anonymizer program and your quick thinking to drop offline, you did a good job of covering your tracks. I should be able to finish it up and make it so no one knows exactly where you are. They probably know you headed south initially, but after you got on the interstate and turned off your implant, they lost you. After that, we jacked the car's identifier system so they probably have no idea where you are."

"Probably doesn't sound certain."

Ramona smiled. "The goons aren't going to find you here, Shelby. This house doesn't exist anymore as far as most of the authorities know. Only the locals know where it is, situated back in the woods the way it is. I've shielded the entire structure so no electromagnetic emanations come off of it. People can't even tell we're using electricity in here. I've tapped into a pretty large stream that runs through the property, creating a small hydro-electric generator that runs all the power in the house. No one knows I'm here and that means no one knows you're here."

That revelation made Shelby feel better. She'd known Ramona was a bit paranoid, but she'd taken her precautions to extremes since the last time Shelby had seen her.

"Go ahead and finish up your waffle. The other will be done soon. Then we can get to work."

Shelby nodded and went back to eating. Ramona wasn't much for talking most of the time and it appeared she'd reached her limit for now. That was fine with Shelby. She wasn't interested in talking anymore either. Her thoughts returned to Cass, wondering what she was up to that afternoon.

Once the two cousins finished breakfast and put the dishes away, Shelby followed Ramona into her office, or "the war room" as she put it. The computer system set up Ramona had was quite impressive.

Shelby had seen a lot of hacker rigs in her day, but this one was over the top. It looked like Ramona had several different completely separate systems running simultaneously. She sat down in front of a bank of computer monitors. There were a half dozen in all, stacked on top of each other in two horizontal rows of three. Three separate mechanical keyboards sat on the desk below each pair of screens in the monitor bank.

Ramona sat down and began typing away at the left-most one. "I'm opening up a connection to the system for you. Open up your implant and search for something called *Ramona one*. It's in my local network here at the house. Be careful. Don't reach out to the Mantle by accident."

"I know what I'm doing. I got this far, didn't I?"

"Sorry. It's just a standard warning. I've forgotten where I am in the process. It happens. I'm always careful and double check things. I'm going to make sure you're cautious, too."

Shelby checked her implant's signal and opened up only enough so she connected to the house's network. Once she was there, she found the port Ramona had mentioned. "I found it, now what?"

"Go ahead and download the cleanest copy of the video

directly to me. I don't wanna pull it off the web because it will have been corrupted from other sources. Getting it straight from you will give me the closest to the original copy there is, and I can get a reading on what they might be able to figure out based on it."

Shelby went ahead and did as she was instructed, downloading the video to Ramona's system. The connection was pretty fast and it was done in a few seconds. Shelby pulled a chair over from the corner and sat down next to Ramona, watching her start working on the complex system she'd created.

"What's next?"

Ramona smiled. "I'm running a system check on the video first. Then I'm going to put it through a series of identifier programs I've created. While they're running in the background, I'm going to scrub your back trail for you and make sure no one can trace you to anywhere near here."

Shelby watched as her cousin continued to work for almost an hour.

Ramona muttered something under her breath, then hit return on the central keyboard one last time, and leaned back in her chair. She stretched her arms up over her head.

"Finished. Right now, Shelby, I can say with some confidence that no one has any clue where you are at this moment. I was even able to go back and wipe your passage through the tolls below Boston. I can't believe how easy it was to break into that system. There's a chance the others might have already pulled that information for themselves, but if they didn't, they aren't going to find it now."

"So that's it? I've just disappeared?"

Ramona nodded, beaming with pride. She held her hand palm out in front of Shelby's forehead and shouted out like a holovid preacher on Sunday morning. "You are Clean!"

The two cousins enjoyed a brief chuckle together before Ramona turned back to the wall of monitors. "Now comes the tricky part. Enough people are looking for you right now that I can't just do my normal scrub and replace job to create you a new identity. They have surely uploaded your likeness into the cloud and are running a facial recognition search for you right now."

Ramona pointed to a series of photographs of Shelby that popped up onto the rightmost screen. "I'm going to have to carefully remove mentions of you, including all these search reference photos, one at a time in a variety of different places. We have to make sure I'm not creating a pattern of deletions that anyone can identify. The goal is to make it so that you just sort of ghost away off the grid without anyone noticing. That's going to take us most of the rest of the day. You can help by running me through your normal daily routine and giving me access to all your accounts at home and at school. Once that's done, I can start passing through those systems and purging them so you were never there."

Shelby nodded. "I can download a GPS track of my location for the last month from my implant. Will that help?"

"That's perfect. Go ahead and upload it to the system named *Ramona three*."

Shelby smiled and started uploading the information to the network port so that Ramona had access to it. While she was doing that, a chime sounded from the system on the left. That was the one running the check on the video.

Ramona leaned close to the lower left monitor, scanning the code displayed there.

"Uh-oh," Ramona said.

"What do you mean, 'uh-oh?'"

"I mean there might be a way to trace the video back to Cass. Where did she get her implant put in?"

"I told you, it was after an accident during a trip we were on. A hospital in the islands installed it."

"Yeah, I remember you telling me about that, but I'd forgotten. It seems as if her system ID's serial number tagged itself to the video. It's deep in the code, but it's there."

"What does that mean?"

"Unless you tell it not to or shut it off permanently, every implant tags its serial number to outgoing transmissions. It's just another way to keep things straight in the Mantle. A lot of people know to shut that off. You probably did it a long time ago. I suspect no one even told Cass about it, and because of that, it's still tagged to the video. It's clearly identified as a medical grade device ID."

Shelby scratched her head. "So?"

"So, that's the problem."

Shelby leaned over and looked at the screen, trying to discern what Ramona was looking at in the lines of computer code.

Ramona pointed at the screen and continued. "The medical ID is tagged back to its manufacturer. All they have to do is find out where that device was sold and where the doctor was who installed it. Then they can hack the medical records and figure out whose implant it is. The good news is, you said you were both down in the islands, right?"

Shelby nodded.

Ramona smiled. "That might actually work in our favor. I think I'll try and see if I can hack in down there, too. We've got to see if we can erase the connection between that medical ID and Cass. I fear it'll be next to impossible to remove all the links. If we can't, then you're going to have to go find a way to get her out of the enclave before they trace it back to her. It's not a matter of if they do it, only when."

Shelby shook her head. "We can't count on being able to get her out of there. Let's get to work and see if we can backtrack it and erase the records. We can do that first. I think it's more important than erasing me right now. We know I'm hidden. Cass is not."

Chapter 20

WHEN CASS and her sister got home, she wanted to go upstairs and try out Cadence's chip update right away. Unfortunately, her mom had stuff for both she and Elena to do around the house that afternoon. By the time she was done with the chores, it was dinner time.

While they sat eating, Cass's mom and dad made random small talk about their day and shared some gossip from the neighborhood. Cass tuned it out. All she could focus on was getting upstairs and running the update to see if she could reach out to Shelby somehow.

She thought she'd finally get away to her room as the family finished their meals, when her dad announced, "I think we should all do something as a family. I want to head out and go down to the Community Center together. I think given everything that's happened since Cass has been back from school, it would be good for people to see us together."

Something about the way he said it irked Cass. "What do you mean, Dad?"

"It's just that everyone here knows about your relationship with that girl."

"Her name is Shelby."

Her dad continued without acknowledging Cass's correction. "I think it's important for people to see that you haven't changed. They need to know you're still the Cass they knew before you went away. That's important, honey. Otherwise, the enclave leadership might decide you're a risk to the community and ask you to leave."

Cass suppressed the smile that she wanted to show, when she heard his mention of the threat every enclave parent held over their teens. Once someone was shunned by the movement, there was no return and no contact.

In this case, shunning would solve her problem. If the other leaders of the community kicked her out, her father would probably try to stop it. He had some standing in the national movement as well as locally, but if he didn't fight it then she'd be free to leave and he wouldn't be able to stop her. Her only other option was to sneak out in the night and get away before anyone could come after her.

It was someone coming after her that Cass feared the most. Her dad wielded a lot of power inside the national Sapiens community. Everyone knew how connected he was to Sterling Noble, the movement's leader. Her father would resist Cass's desire to go back to school any way he could. He would fear the embarrassment her defection would cause him.

Cass decided her only recourse right now was to nod and smile at his request to go out. She had to ignore the slight to Shelby. She couldn't very well refuse, not until she had some sort of plan to get away. Otherwise, he'd just come out and get her. He had friends inside the local police force so she couldn't rely on them to help her if she told someone she was in danger.

After dinner, the four of them left the house together and walked through the neighborhood towards the enclave's Recreation and Community Center. According to the digital sign in front of the building, a movie had been planned for that evening's activity. It was an old two-dimensional flat screen version of a classic comedy that happened to be one of her father's favorites when he was a kid. She'd seen it at least four times growing up, but decided to make the best of it and enjoy the show.

Cass surprised herself at how much she enjoyed the movie. It was called Home Alone, and it was about a boy celebrating an old Christian holiday, in which his parents left him home with no supervision. It was cute and pretty funny in a weird sort of way. Her father laughed louder than anyone else.

When the movie ended, Cass got up and walked over to the refreshment table to get something to drink. She picked up one of the sugar cookies laid out with all the other snacks.

Nick Glenn stepped up beside her as she took a bite. "It's nice to see you out and about in the community again, Cassie."

"Oh, hi, Nick. I didn't realize you were here. I'm sorry I didn't get back in touch with you sooner. It's been a little hectic at my house and I've had some trouble adjusting to being home again. I'm sure you understand."

"Yeah, I've had the same issues. Our parents don't seem to understand that we went away and lived independently for three or four months. Now that we're home again, they expect us to come back and be the little kids we were before."

Cass smiled in spite of everything that occupied her mind. "Exactly, Nick. You nailed it."

After an awkward silence, Nick cleared his throat and said, "Hey, Cass, I wanted to apologize for that little ambush party my parents threw the first day you were back. I didn't want to do it, but they kind of forced me. It was a total jerk move."

"It's all right. I kind of figured out what it was pretty quickly. I decided to go along with it for at least a little while and get a chance to see everyone."

"Yeah, well everyone in the community was a little worried about you when your parents told us about that girl you were living with."

Cass stiffened at the tone Nick used when he referred to Shelby.

"That girl isn't what anybody thinks she is, Nick. You know me and what kind of person I am. She's not some sort of monster who somehow mind-controlled me if that's what you're worried about. She's a girl just like me who went away to college and made a new friend. That's all."

"Cass, you know that's something someone would say even if they were under mind control."

Cass stared at Nick for a few seconds and then glanced past him, over his shoulder. Nick's mom and dad watched them from across the room.

Seeing them observing Nick talking with her brought all her frustration boiling to the surface. "You apologize for ambushing me at the party my first day back, then you come over here tonight and you do the exact same thing? How is it you didn't think I'd pick up on that?"

"Cass, it's not like that."

Nick's shocked expression made her wonder if she'd overreacted. At that moment, she didn't care enough to backtrack, though.

"No, Nick, I think it is. Go and tell your parents that I'm not some kind of freak. Tell them I'm not under mind control and it turns out Shelby is a lot better friend to me than any of you."

Cass didn't wait for a reply. She turned around and walked back over to where her parents were talking with another couple. Elena was over chatting with Cadence and a few other friends from middle school.

"Dad, I think it's time for me to go. Do you mind if I head back home on my own?"

Her dad started to say something but her mom interrupted him with a hand on his arm. Her mom smiled at her eldest daughter and said, "It would really be nice if you stayed here and mingled a little bit, Cassie."

Cass fumed at being told no, but she'd gotten her answer when she looked to her father and he nodded in agreement.

"Your mother's right, Cass. Talk to your friends and hang around. See, Elena's having a good time. You should do the same thing."

"I don't mind talking to people, Dad, but they're all interrogating me for their parents. Why don't the two of you just ask me the questions you have for me and be done with it. Stop sending all my friends to do it for you."

A sad smile crossed her father's face. "People are worried about you Cass, not just us. You should accept that for what it is — genuine concern for your welfare."

"There's nothing wrong with me, Dad. I've got a new girlfriend, that's all. There's nothing else going on."

Cass felt like she was repeating the same things over and over again. She was tired of having to defend Shelby to these people, including her family. "You know what? I'm just going to go home on my own anyway. I'm over 18 and you can't tell me what to do, no matter what you might think. I'll see you all back at the house."

Cass headed for the nearest exit without waiting for her parents to answer. Once outside, Cass started down the sidewalk, taking a longer, more circuitous route to return home.

A voice called out from behind her. It was Susan.

"Cassie, slow down. I'll walk with you."

Cass snapped an accusing glance at her ex-girlfriend as she caught up to her. "Aren't you afraid you'll catch my disease?"

"That's not fair. I'm not like all the others, Cass. It's me. We're not going out anymore, but you can still trust me."

Cass wasn't sure she could trust anyone here anymore, not even Susan. She didn't say anything, though. Instead, she kept walking, but moved to one edge of the sidewalk to make room for Susan to walk beside her.

As they ambled, Susan chattered away about her time at school. Cass didn't pay close attention, but it was hard not to listen. Susan had found a new girlfriend and seemed happy enough based on what she said. The surprising admission came when she said she wasn't thrilled with the options available to her from the enclave's college programs.

"Sue, if you want to go to the University, just tell your parents you want to go there."

"It's not that easy, Cass. After what happened with you, everyone's leery of letting their kids veer away from approved programs."

Cass cursed and threw her hands in the air. "Dammit, I'm sick and tired of everybody pretending I'm damaged goods just because I went somewhere else. I'm no different than when I left and it's pissing me off the way everyone's treating me."

Susan smiled and placed a calming hand on Cass's arm. "It's okay, Cass. I'd be pissed, too, in your position. I know you better than anyone around here. I have to admit, when I first heard about you and Shelby, I was a little freaked out. Then I saw you a few weeks ago at Nick's party, and I realized you hadn't changed much at all. I think everyone is wrong about this. Shelby must be really nice if you feel about her the way you seem to."

Susan's words surprised Cass. She didn't say anything in response, though. The pair walked on along the darkened residential streets in silence for a while.

As they approached the street where Sue lived, Cass said, "Sue, I think I want to walk the rest away by myself. Is that all right? I appreciate everything you said. I just need some time alone right now."

Sue looked like she was about to say something, but then she stopped herself. She leaned in and gave Cass a hug, then turned and walked down the street towards her home.

Cass decided she wasn't ready to face her parents yet, so instead, she took the turn towards the bike trail that led through the enclave's small wooded nature preserve. There was a favorite spot there just off the path that would allow her to be alone with her thoughts for a little bit.

As Cass headed into the woods on the bike trail, she pulled out her phone and sent her parents a brief text message. It was strange using her thumbs to do it rather than composing it via her implant.

Mom and Dad, I'm out for an extended walk. I need to think about some things. I'll be home late.

Several hours later, Cass stared up at the clear night sky and sighed. Her breath billowed out in a tiny vapor cloud due to the chill of winter weather. Cass decided to get up from where she sat on a fallen log in the woods and head home. She'd needed the peaceful-ness that came from listening to the quiet burble of the stream nearby and the slight breeze in the trees. Cass might have been tempted to spend the night here alone if it weren't for the damp chill that settled over the area this time of year.

Cass had always found it was an excellent place to collect her thoughts when she couldn't find a way through a difficult time in her life. She used to come here with Susan all the time and it held many fond memories. Now, all she wanted was to share it with Shelby, too.

Her thoughts reached out and Cass wished she could somehow telepathically communicate with Shelby without using her implant. She decided she needed to head back and try to use Cadence's chip to break through the security system. She'd left it at home when she walked to the Rec Center earlier with her family.

Cass started back towards her house, arriving 15 minutes later. It was after eleven o'clock. As she turned up her driveway, Cass realized most of the house was dark. Her parents had already gone to bed without staying up to wait for her. Relief flowed over her, relaxing muscles tensed for a potential confrontation. Cass didn't want to deal with her parents right now.

She was just about to reach for the kitchen doorknob when it opened and Elena almost bumped into her as she was coming out.

"Elena, what the hell are you doing sneaking out this time of night?"

"Oh, Cass. I figured since someone spotted you leaving with Susan that maybe you were staying over at her place tonight. That was what Mom and Dad hoped anyway."

"Why would I stay there? Susan's not my girlfriend anymore."

"I know, but…"

"No. Stop trying to change the subject. What are you doing sneaking out of the house again? I thought we discussed this the last time."

"Cass, you're not the boss of me or anyone else. You're not Mom or Dad and you can't tell me what to do."

"Elena, you're not being responsible. Who is it you're going to hang out with tonight?"

"Phil."

When Cass's mouth dropped open to say something, Elena

jumped in to add, "He really cares for me, Cass, not that you'd understand that."

"Of course, I understand, Elena. I told you I've dealt with boys like that before. Phil and the others like him are only after you for sex. He doesn't care about you, Elena. You're too young to be hanging around someone as old as he is anyway."

Elena tried to push past her sister to reach the driveway but Cass grabbed her shoulder and pulled her back into the kitchen, closing the door. Cass turned around and stood there, blocking the way.

Elena shook off Cass's grasp. "Let go of me."

"I'm not letting you go to hang out with Phil tonight, Elena. Give it up. I caught you. Now go back to bed. We'll talk about this tomorrow."

"I'm not listening to you, Cass. You've got your own problems. Stop worrying about what I'm doing all the time."

Elena's voice had raised in volume throughout the argument. Cass glanced down the hallway behind her sister, afraid that their parents would wake up.

"Keep your voice down. Unless you want Mom and Dad coming out here to find you completely dressed to go out. I don't think you want that."

"I don't care. Let them come. It's about time they understood that I'm as grown-up as you are."

Cass winced as Elena's voice got louder. She really sounded like she wanted their parents waking up. It was insane.

Cass lowered her voice in an attempt to quiet her sister down. "Elena, you're not making sense. Look, I just want you to be safe and not take unnecessary risks. That's all."

"I don't understand why you can't be cool with me when I'm perfectly okay with all of your freaky stuff. I keep your secrets. Why can't you keep mine?"

"There's a difference between secrets like mine and you doing something that could hurt you."

Elena rolled her eyes. "I'm not going to get hurt, Cass. I've been with boys before, lots. I know how to take care of myself."

"I don't care how experienced you think you are, Elena. You're not going to convince me that it's a good idea to sneak out with Phil tonight. If you think it's all right, why do you have to sneak around? Tell Mom and Dad and go on a real date with him if that's what you want."

Elena shrieked and flung herself at Cass, pushing her sister back against the cabinets in the kitchen as she made a break for the kitchen door. Cass caught herself with a hand on the counter, regained her balance, and reached out to grab Elena as she went by.

When she grabbed Elena's arm again, a voice sounded behind her. "What the hell is going on in here, girls?" Her father asked. "You woke your mother and me with all the noise."

Both Cass's mother and father stood in the doorway to the kitchen that led to the rest of the house.

Despite being angry at her sister, Cass didn't want to tell on her. "Dad, Elena and I were just having an argument. It was just stupid sister stuff, that's all."

"No, it wasn't that, Mom and Dad. Cass here didn't want me to go out and meet up with a boy I like."

Her mom reacted first to Elena's revelation. "Why were you going out to meet a boy at this hour? You know the rules."

"I'm old enough to make my own decisions, Mom. You have to stop treating me like a little girl. Besides which, I'm the most responsible one in the family now, not Cassie."

Their father put his hands on his hips. "What's that supposed to mean?"

"It just means that I'm not taking the risks that Cass is and you should be happy I'm not like her."

"Elena, shut up," Cass snapped.

"Or what? Are you afraid I'm going to say something to Mom and Dad about anything in particular?"

Cass blanched at the open threat. She knew what her sister was getting at. "Stop it, stop it right now."

Cass glared at her sister. She didn't know how to end this, but she was afraid of what Elena was going to do or say if she kept getting angrier.

"I'm tired of you ordering me around, Cass. I've kept your

secret and I'm tired of keeping it." Elena turned to her parents and pointed at Cass. "Do you know your perfect older daughter has a cyber implant in the side of her head? She's a damned sub and you didn't even know it!"

"Elena!" Cass yelled. Her mind whirled, trying to find a way out of this horrible situation. "How could you?"

"You can't keep my secrets, then I can't keep yours."

Her dad turned towards Cass. "Cassie, what is Elena talking about? She's kidding, right?"

Cass met her father's questioning eyes but couldn't bring herself to answer him. She struggled with whether she should lie and try to cover up what was going on, or come clean and own up to it. Maybe telling her parents everything would get her kicked out of the enclave quicker.

Her mother took a step towards Cass. "Answer your father. We're your parents and we deserve an answer from you Cass. None of this is true, right? You didn't do something foolish and mutilate your body, did you?"

"So, what if I did?"

Her father stepped forward, gripping Cass's shoulder with one hand and reaching out with his other to grasp her chin. He tilted her head back-and-forth looking at Cass's face. "Elena, I don't see anything. Why would you say something so horrible about your sister."

Cass shot a pleading glare at her sister to stop this whole thing.

Elena sneered and pointed at Cass. "Go ahead. Tell him, Cassie. Tell him how you have your face covered up with fake skin."

Cass realized they'd reached a point of no return. Elena wasn't going to back down.

Cass took a step back from her father. "Mom, Dad, it's not something I wanted to do. There was an accident and when I woke up, the doctors had already done it."

Her father's glare hardened. "What doctors, Cass? When was this accident?"

"When I went on my trip to the Bahamas. There was a horrible accident when we were racing jet skis. I got hurt and was taken to the hospital. They told me I almost died but the doctors were able to reverse the injury to my brain with an implant. That's all it is, Dad. It doesn't do anything bad to me, it just keeps me alive."

Cass realized she had to show them everything. She reached up and tapped the corners of her skin patch until the edge peeled up. She grasped the intersection between her forefinger and thumb and lifted the patch away from her face, revealing the metal implant extending from just beyond her eye back to her ear.

Her mother started sobbing and looked away as soon as Cass revealed the implant to them.

Her dad reached out as if he was about to touch it, but then pulled his hand away. Instead, he said, "Cass, how could you?"

"I told you, Dad. It was an accident and I had no control over it. The implant was already there when I woke up at the hospital."

"You should've called us right away. We could've had doctors from the enclave, from the movement, come down and assess you. The medical device companies and cybernetics firms push doctors to use implants over other potential treatments. Doctors listen to them because they don't want to do real medicine anymore, they just want their tech and cyber solutions to take care of everything for them."

"Dad, it doesn't matter either way. It's in me now and there's nothing anyone can do. I tried to get them to remove it when I woke up. They told me it would kill me or turn me into a vegetable if they did that."

Her father shook his head, his voice stern. "We'll see about that. I want one of the enclave's doctors to examine you. I'm sure there's something that can be done that those island hacks didn't tell you about. For now, just go up to your room. I don't want to see you and that thing on your face anymore."

He turned his gaze to Elena. "You're not out of trouble, either, young lady. You go to your room, too. We'll talk about this with both of you in the morning."

Cass glared at Elena, then marched past her parents. Cass's mother flinched away from her when she came close. Cass didn't even care. She was too angry with Elena to worry about her parents' reaction to her cybernetics.

Cass headed into her room and slammed her door for the first time since she was Elena's age. She dove onto her bed and began to cry.

Chapter 21

CASS RESISTED the urge to flinch or even lean away from the doctor's probing fingers. She didn't like people touching her face under normal circumstances. Since her accident, that aversion had magnified, especially for the area around her implant. That was magnified when that person was the enclave's physician. He was a medical doctor but also a loyal Sapiens Movement member. As such, he was as devoted to the cause as anyone else living in the enclave. Cass couldn't help but feel like he was examining her the way he might analyze some sort of strange medical experiment.

The last five days had showed how much the fears of her parents' reaction to her implant were on target. It was as if Cass had been under house arrest. She spent most of her time alone in her room. She wasn't talking to Elena at all anymore, and neither of her parents said anything to her other than to let her know when her meals were ready.

Cass couldn't even try to use the chip Cadence had made for her so she could reach out and contact Shelby. Elena must have told her parents about it under further questioning, because her father came up that first night and demanded it from her before she could activate the update it contained. That was the final blow that made her realize how isolated she was from everything and everyone she'd ever cared about.

This was her first time out of the house since revealing her implants to her parents. It took her father this long to arrange an appointment after getting answers to his detailed questions about her accident a few months before and the subsequent medical treatment.

Doctor Sanders turned to Cass's father. He hadn't addressed Cass at all other than what was necessary to position her for the exam. "The work here is actually quite excellent, James. I wouldn't have expected that from a doctor in the islands."

"So, it's not some kind of botched procedure?" Cass's father asked. "That gives us a better chance of reversing it, right?"

"It's not botched at all. On the contrary, everything appears to be well managed. There's almost no scarring visible anywhere around the implant itself. They must've had excellent facilities and resources, given the location."

Doctor Sanders moved around to stand in front of Cass and addressed her directly. "Do you have any residual pain around the surgical site or headaches or anything else unusual?"

Cass shook her head. "No."

She kept her eyes focused directly ahead, staring at the wall. She answered in a monotone, trying not to display any emotion at all in the face of the humiliating and invasive physical exam that the doctor had performed. Cass's father and mother had insisted the Doctor assure them there were no other hidden implants they couldn't see. The whole process had been horrible.

Now they got to the real reason why her parents had brought her here. They wanted to find out when they could remove the implants in their daughter's head. Cass already knew the answer to that question. She'd told them numerous times, though they never believed her and had stopped listening to her.

Cass's father gestured to his daughter. "So, Doc, what's your opinion? When can you get that thing out of my little girl's head?"

"It's not something I want to rush into. Don't get me wrong, James. I can do the procedure you're requesting. I completely understand the urgent need to get it done. However, I want you and Faye to understand that I believe there will be a significant loss of function once it's removed."

Cass turned from staring at the wall. She directed her glare at her parents and the doctor. "Some limitation of function? I'll be damned near comatose or dead if this thing is taken out of me, not to mention blind in one eye and deaf on one side."

Her father shot her a stern look. "Cass, you speak to the doctor with respect. He's doing this as a favor to me without telling anyone else about it. If this kind of thing gets out, you'll be out on your ass. I'm trying to save your life here."

"No, Dad, you're not. You're trying to save your reputation. You're more worried that you, Mom, and Elena will get kicked out with me."

Her father started to say something in response then closed his mouth and turned back to Doctor Sanders. "So, you can remove it?"

"Oh, most certainly. The trick will be removing it while maintaining as much function as possible. I'm sorry for the lack of certainty about the final outcome. We can take anything out, it's a problem of replacing the functionality that was removed to install it. They excised a significant portion of your daughter's brain to make room for the implant."

Her mother started sobbing as she muttered, "Butchers."

Cass bit back a response. She'd explained all this to her father and mother already. She'd even given them permission to contact the hospital in the Caribbean via a signed release letter so they could see the full extent of her injuries. They all knew as well as she did that the part of her brain that was removed was damaged beyond any normal surgical repair.

Her dad shook his head and sighed. "All right, I guess that's it. Thanks, Doc. When can we set up the procedure?"

Cass turned to face the three of them, her mouth hanging open, unable to speak. They'd heard everything she'd heard and their only conclusion was to try and kill her? She had no more words for any of them. Cass could only sit and listen as the doctor answered her father.

"That's going to be an issue, James. It'll probably be three to five days, maybe even a week."

Her dad frowned. "Why so long?"

"Because I need to assemble a reliable team to assist me. This is going to be a little tricky and delicate. Most hospitals do this with advanced robotics. Obviously, we aren't going to do that here, so I'm going to need extra pairs of hands. It's not going to be cheap, either. If it were just me, I'd do it for the cost of a normal out-patient procedure. The others I hire will require enough money to keep them quiet about what we've done."

Her dad paused in thought, then said, "All right, go ahead and do what you need to do. She's not going anywhere. We'll be ready whenever you tell us to come."

Cass's father looked at her and pointed to the doctor. "Say thank you, Cassie. He's doing us a favor."

Cass glared at her father. "No. He's not doing me any favors. He's violating his oath to do no harm and he knows it. That's why he has to pay off his surgical team to keep them quiet."

She hopped off the exam table and walked towards the door. "May I leave now?"

Her father pointed to her face. "First, cover that thing up."

Cass smirked at the hypocrisy of it all and pulled out the skin patch from its case in her pocket, placing it back on her face so it covered the implant again.

"Now can I go?"

"Wait, your mother and I are coming with you," Her dad said.

"Still afraid I'm going to run away and embarrass you?"

"Cass, you don't know what you're thinking right now. It's the machine making all the decisions for you."

"That's ridiculous, Dad. I'm not even hooked into the Mantle right now. How is the machine making any decisions for me if that's the case? I'm able to make my own decisions and I don't want you removing this implant from my head."

Her dad shook his head. "You're delirious. Let's get you home and back to your room so you can rest." He reached out and grabbed her by the upper arm to bring her along with him.

Cass twisted her shoulder away, pulling her arm out of his grasp. "I can walk fine on my own without you dragging me home like I need to be on some kind of leash."

Cass marched out of the doctor's office. She'd never been so angry in her life. She couldn't believe her father and mother were actually considering going through with this procedure. At best it was going to leave her a drooling vegetable. They didn't even care as long as it kept the family's reputation whole.

Followed by her parents, Cass walked to the car and climbed in the back. They all drove back across the enclave to the residential part of the community. The enclave's small medical center was well-equipped, but it wasn't a full-service hospital by any stretch of the imagination. The thought of getting brain surgery there frightened Cass more than she could bear.

Once home, they all got out of the car in the driveway. Cass's father pointed to the car parked on the street in front of their house. "Someone's here. I wonder who it could be."

Cass shrugged. "Who cares? Maybe it's one of Elena's new boyfriends. She probably took advantage of us being away to get some on the side."

"That's enough of that, Cassidy," Her dad snapped. "Go up to your room. I'll have your mother call you when it's dinner time. Until then, you can sit up there and think about how you've shamed this family."

Cass spun around and held her head up as she marched into the house. She wasn't going to let them know how much all of this beat down her spirit.

Cass started towards the stairs, her intent to go up to her bedroom without talking to anyone. Her plans fell through when she bumped into Simon Cantwell standing in the hallway talking to her sister.

The Sapiens First leader smiled down at her. "Well, hello, Cassidy. You're just the person I wanted to talk to. Your sister here was explaining to me a little bit about your current problem. It's funny because that is also why I came back."

Cass's father came into the house and walked into the hallway. "Simon, what are you doing here?"

"I came back to see your elder daughter. She has some information I think I need for my investigation."

Her dad seemed confused. "What sort of information. How could she know anything about that video or the people who recorded and disseminated it?"

Simon showed his teeth in a feral grin. "Because, James, your daughter is the one who recorded that video. It was her sub girlfriend who then streamed it live to the Mantle for everyone to see."

Her father turned and stared at Cass. His mouth hung open in shock, unable to speak.

Cass's mother had come into the hallway. It was apparent she also heard what Simon said.

Cass met her mother's hurt gaze, pleading with her eyes for help.

Her mom looked away and turned around. "Excuse me. I think I'm going to leave now. This is obviously something for the two of you to handle."

Cass's heart plunged into her gut. Her mother had abandoned her, leaving her in the hands of her father and this murderer. Her mom clearly wanted no part of whatever the two men planned on doing with her.

Her father spoke, breaking the silence left by her mother's departure. "Cass, I believe you should come with Mr. Cantwell and me into my office. I think you have some explaining you need to do. You've heard us talking about this video the whole time you were here, and yet you said nothing. Why?"

Cass didn't answer. She walked past her father down the hallway to his office. Simon and her father followed right behind her. She knew she needed to figure out a way to escape but right now, there was no way she'd make it past the two men. Even if she did, where would she go? She didn't have any plan to escape the enclave.

When they reached the office, her father pointed to one of the chairs arranged in front of his antique wooden desk. "Sit down, Cass. I want you to answer my questions."

Cass sat in one of the padded leather wingback chairs situated in front of her father's desk. He went around the desk and sat down opposite her. Simon moved in and stood to one side, placed so he could look at both of them.

Cass shrugged. "I don't know what you want me to say. You and Simon here…You don't mind if I call you Simon, do you?"

The Sapiens First leader nodded in her direction. "You're an adult and I plan on treating you like one, so you may call me whatever you wish."

His stare made Cass's skin crawl and she quickly looked away, back to her father as she continued. "You and Simon here have been talking as if the events on that video never happened. I think we can agree that all three of us now know how horribly authentic it really is."

Cass glanced up at Simon. "Given that information, what could I possibly add to your investigation, Simon, when you are obviously only interested in trying to cover up the murder of the seven individuals you killed on that stage?"

Cass turned back to her father again. "One of them was Shelby's brother, Eric. Did you know that, Dad?"

Her father nodded. "I did. He got himself into that position. None of the subs should have been anywhere near that rally. I made sure the police chief got some officers friendly to the movement to warn him to stay away. I can't be held responsible when he didn't take the hint."

"This isn't his fault, Dad. It's Simon's." Cass pointed at the Sapiens First leader. "You wore a mask on that stage, but I recognized your voice as soon as you came into our home. The tattoo on your forearm is quite distinctive, by the way."

Cass didn't know where all this bravado was coming from. She certainly didn't feel it deep inside, but she didn't know what else to do. If she didn't stand up to them, they were going to try and force her to do whatever it was they wanted. She had to be brave and strong. She couldn't give up Shelby's location, no matter what they did to her.

As if in response to her thoughts, Simon leaned over the desk, placing both his hands flat on the broad wooden top so he could look directly into Cass's eyes. "Cass, you're already in a lot of trouble. However, your father is placed high enough in the organization that if you cooperate now, I think we can both agree that the punishment will be rather light, considering the level of your betrayal to humanity. On the other hand, if you do not comply with my request for information, then I'm afraid there's nothing your father will be able to do to protect you from what must inevitably happen."

Despite feeling like she was going to burst into tears at any moment, Cass held Simon's hard gaze for a few seconds before she said, "What, Simon, are you planning to kill me, too, with that thing hanging in the Benson's house?"

Simon sneered, which told her he knew exactly what she was talking about. Dammit, they were all in on it, even her father.

Simon pulled a small notebook from his coat pocket and said, "Cass, I'm going to ask you a few questions. Understand this. I'm only going to ask them once. If you don't answer, or answer incorrectly, I won't be responsible for what will happen to you after that. Only out of respect to your father do I even offer a sub like you anything approaching humane treatment."

"Daddy, are you going to let him do this to me?"

Her father stared at her for a few seconds, then looked away. "This falls under Simon's jurisdiction now, Cassie. I'm sorry, but you got yourself into this mess. I'm afraid you'll have to get yourself out of it."

Simon nodded. "Thank you, James. Now, Cass, there's no use denying that you were the one that took the video. We know you did because we were able to trace the serial number of the implant that recorded it back to the medical device manufacturer. They keep quite good records and for the right payoff, the corporate librarian was only too happy to provide us the information we needed. After that, it was simple to follow the trail to the hospital where it was installed. You can imagine my surprise when I found your name at the end of our search. That was quite a nasty accident you were in down there, by the way."

"So what?" Cass asked. "I guess I'm supposed to applaud you for your detective work?"

"No, I'm merely telling you what we know so you are aware of how thorough we are. I will know if you're lying to me so let's avoid any unpleasantness and tell me what you know. We know you've been in touch with that sub girlfriend of yours. We were able to track some transmissions coming out of this enclave that went to a net address she used before she went dark. What did you two talk about?"

"I'm not telling you that. Ask me something else."

"I told you not to mislead me, Cass,"

"I'm not misleading you, Simon. I told you that I wasn't going to answer your question. That's not lying, it's just not answering."

Simon sighed and set his notebook down. As he started to remove his sport coat and rolled up the sleeves of his white dress shirt, he said, "James, I think maybe you should leave the room."

Cass's father hesitated. "I am not sure about that, Simon."

"I'm afraid I must insist. I'm going to have to convince your daughter to listen to reason. It'll be better if you're not here to see or hear it."

"You're not going to do anything permanently damaging to her, are you?"

Cass shot a horrified glance at her father. He was going to leave her alone with this butcher. "How could you even consider letting him be alone with me, Daddy?"

"I'm sorry, Cassidy. You could've just answered his questions as he asked. Like I said earlier, this falls under his jurisdiction and I have absolutely no control over what happens anymore."

Tears welled up in her eyes as her father stood up and left the room, pulling the door closed behind him, abandoning her to whatever Simon planned to do next.

Simon reached down to where he'd hung his coat over the back of a chair. He pulled out a small rectangular box. "Now we can get down to business."

The grey metal box had a few round black buttons on it, a dial set below a tiny LED screen, and a flimsy, rubberized wire antenna coming out of one end. Cass watched as Simon fiddled with some of the settings before holding it up and looking at the readout on the tiny screen.

"This, Cass, is a nasty little device we came up with to use when convincing subs like yourself to cooperate with us. One of the nice things about your primary implant is that it gives us direct neural access to various centers of your brain. For instance, if I wanted to, I could reward you by accessing your brain's pleasure centers.

Before Cass could react, a flood of total body stimulation washed over her. It was unlike anything she'd ever felt before. The intensity of the sensations made it so all she could do was let out a small gasp as she sunk deeper into her seat. Her hands trembled as she gripped the padded arms of the chair while Simon held down the button.

He smiled as he stood there watching Cass writhe in the chair. "I want to prove to you that I can do what I say I can do." Simon let go of the button and the sudden stimulation went away. Cass found herself hugging her arms across her chest, breathing heavily, soaked in a cold sweat.

"Under the right circumstances, stimulating the pleasure centers can eventually become almost as painful as some of the other alternatives I have at my command. Like this one."

Simon reached out again, holding the box next to her implant and thumbing the switch once more. This time, it felt like every nerve in her body had been set on fire. Every inch of Cass's skin and bones burned with the most intense agony she'd ever felt. She couldn't even scream because the muscles in her abdomen that controlled her breathing were frozen in pain. It seemed to go on forever.

Simon released the button again and pulled his arm away. Just as quickly as it had appeared, the pain left her. She remembered it, though. She'd never forget what that burning pain felt like.

Cass gasped for air, as she tried to catch her breath after her respiratory muscles had been frozen for so long.

As she did, she glared up at Simon. "I don't care what you do to me, you bastard. I'm not going to tell you where Shelby is. I can't, because I don't know. Like you said, we talked and then she went dark. I haven't talked to her since."

"Maybe, and then again, maybe not. Let's play a little game, Cassidy. I'll ask you a question. If you get it right, you get a little jolt of pleasure. If you get it wrong… Well, I'll give you more than just a jolt of the alternative. Choose carefully because there are no take backs."

Cass gripped the arms of the chair and stared deep into Simon's eyes. She thought maybe if she held onto something like the anger and desire to cause him the kind of pain he created in her, it would help get her through what happened next. Cass soon discovered she was wrong, but she kept trying anyway. No matter what, she wouldn't willingly give up anything she knew about Shelby.

Chapter 22

CASS GROANED as she rolled over in bed. She didn't know what to do and whether she should cry or scream or what. Simon had been very thorough in his questioning of her. It felt like it had lasted for hours, though she'd lost track of everything around her after the tenth time he'd pressed the button on his infernal machine. The man always knew just how to work at it until she finally gave up and answered him.

Cass hugged her arms to her chest and sobbed, "Shelby, I hope you forgive me."

She'd eventually given up what she knew of Shelby's planned destination at her cousin's house. Cass didn't know the cousin's name, but apparently, that was enough information for Simon. He'd asked a few more questions after she'd given up Shelby's location, but it seemed as if he was just enjoying the torture at that point. When he'd let her go, he'd ordered her to stand up and leave the office, telling her to go to her room. He'd told her he'd planned on coming back and asking her more questions later. She'd wanted to run away, but instead had followed his commands to the letter and started up to her room.

As soon as Cass had left her father's office and turned toward the stairs, she'd noticed two men she'd never seen before standing by the front door in the hallway. The one on the right had glared at her as she'd come around the corner, nudging the other to draw his partner's attention to her presence. Cass had realized they must be with Simon. They had been part of his Sapiens First security team or something like it. It had been evident to her they'd been there to guard against her escape, and possibly her family's, too.

She hadn't said anything, keeping her eyes down as she'd shuffled past them. Every part of her body had ached or burned or something. She hadn't known if she'd ever feel right again.

Cass had climbed the stairs, taking each step one at a time until she'd been able to make it to the top and had been able to get into her room where she'd collapsed onto her bed. Now, all she could think about was where Shelby was and if Simon had been able to obtain enough information to track her down or not.

Shelby was street-wise and smart, Cass knew, but that didn't mean she was up to evading someone with the resources Simon had at his disposal. She had to get a warning to Shelby, somehow, but it had been days since she'd talked to her. As she ticked the days off in her mind, Cass realized it had been almost a week since the two of them had last spoken. Shelby could be anywhere at this point and that was a good thing. All Cass could hope as exhaustion overwhelmed her, was that Shelby wasn't with her cousin.

A tap at Cass's door woke her later that afternoon. It was already getting dark in Cass's room. She hadn't turned on the light before she'd fallen asleep. She didn't bother to get up and turn it on now, even though the sun was starting to go down.

"Cassie," her mother said from outside the door. "It's dinner time. You need to come down and eat something. Once you do that, you can come back up here to rest."

Those were the same words her mother had said to her three times a day since she'd found out about Cass's implants. She'd said nearly the same thing every time and that was the extent of their interaction.

Cass got up. She felt a little better after some sleep and her muscles didn't ache quite so much. She wouldn't be running any marathons anytime soon though. She went out the door and was nearly bowled over by Elena, running past her in the hallway.

Her little sister stopped and stared at her for a few seconds. She'd also refused to say anything extra to her big sister. She sneered at Cass, laughed, and ran down the stairs. The two guards still stood by the front door, each of them wearing black trousers and a light windbreaker jacket over top a buttondown shirt. She was sure they were armed in some way. They didn't really need it, though, since both of them were huge and could easily overpower her if she tried to force her way past them.

Cass shuffled into the dining room and sat down at the table. The one good thing about her situation, if she could find a silver lining at all, was that she didn't have to help with dinner or do any of the dishes. She guessed they figured the condemned didn't have to do chores.

Cass sat down and dished up some food from the bowl in front of her onto the plate. She didn't care what it was. She needed the calories after the way her implant had worked overtime during Simon's interrogation. It was some sort of pasta and meat. Cass mechanically shoveled it into her mouth so that she could make sure she didn't run out of energy. It was essential to keep her strength up in case an opportunity to get away presented itself.

After eating her fill, Cass excused herself, stood up, and went back to her bedroom. As she started up the stairs, she overheard her mother start a conversation with Simon back in the dining room. Nobody had said a word while Cass was there. They waited until she left the room before resuming whatever it was they were talking about. Cass didn't care, she turned up her auditory implant and listened in to the entire discussion.

"Simon, I feel like I should feed something to your men."

"That's all right, Faye, they're fine. When their shift relief comes in a few hours, they can go into town and get something to eat on the way back to the motel."

"Well, at least let me get them some coffee or something. They've been standing there all day without moving and I feel like they should be offered some sort of hospitality in my home."

"I'm sure coffee would be appreciated. Thank you, Faye."

Cass stopped listening at that point. Her mother disgusted her. Cass was about to be turned into a vegetable or maybe worse, killed, if the planned procedure was performed. And all her mother could worry about was whether she was a good hostess to the guards who were keeping her trapped here.

Cass got to her room and laid down on the bed. She'd had enough and couldn't bring herself to think about the betrayal by her family anymore. After the questioning from Simon, her body was all too ready to fall into another deep, yet fitful sleep. Cass gave in as the darkness folded over her.

Chapter 23

TWO DAYS LATER DURING BREAKFAST, Cass's father looked up from his phone and said, "I just got some good news. Doctor Sanders messaged me. He's assembled his team a little quicker than he expected. They're available to do the procedure tomorrow."

Cass slumped in her seat. She'd given up trying to fight back anymore. Simon Cantwell had left the morning after he had questioned her but he'd promised to return soon.

Her mom looked up at her husband, seeming to be a little shocked. "So quickly?"

Her father nodded as he glanced at Cass then back to his wife. "I think sooner is better. It's not fair to keep her waiting for a prolonged period. Besides which, I think if we leave her the way she is, Simon is going to want to come back and talk to her again. If we remove her implant, he won't have any reason to visit again."

Cass turned and glared at her father. "I'm surprised you don't just ask him to come back and question me every single day, Daddy. Now that you've let him torture me once, what's to keep you from letting him do it anytime he feels like it?"

"Cassidy, you brought that on yourself. All you had to do was answer his questions. You've carried your betrayal too far. Besides, despite what you may think, I am protecting you. Once the procedure is done, I don't think there'll be any need for Simon to question you."

"Of course, there won't," Cass blurted out. "I'll be a drooling moron missing half my brain. God, how can the two of you sit there and even consider letting that quack do surgery on me? He hasn't seen the inside of a real hospital in years. He's got no business doing brain surgery on a dog, let alone me."

Her father banged his fist on the table. "That's quite enough Cass. If you're finished with your breakfast, go back up to your room and stay there. I'm going to make the arrangements and that's that. We will all say some prayers and hope the procedure is successful. We'll have you back to your normal self before you know it."

Cass bit back a reply. She pushed the chair back, got up, and left the room. A murmur of voices followed her into the hallway as her parents continued their conversation behind her, but she didn't bother to listen in. She was done listening to anything those people had to say. Right now, she knew she had to figure a way out of here before tomorrow morning or she was going to be as good as dead. Cass passed the two Sapiens First thugs Simon had left stationed at the front door. They stood there, close to the bottom of the stairs to guard against Cass's escape.

She considered the two of them as she started up the steps. Almost every scenario she'd come up with so far ended as soon as the guards caught her sneaking out and returned her to her bedroom. No matter what she came up with, Cass couldn't think of a way to get past them without some kind of alert sounding.

Her father had changed the code on the home's alarm system. He activated it every night now, even though there was very little crime inside the enclave itself. The alarm was set so that Cass couldn't get out through her window or via the back door. Its purpose now was to keep her in, not burglars out.

As she thought about her chances to get away, the first part of any plan was to find a way to get past the guards. Secondly, she had to get past the alarm. The third thing involved finding a way out of the enclave without any of the cameras spotting her or tripping the firewall and security wards on the perimeter. Only once she made it outside, could Cass tackle the nearly impossible task of finding Shelby before Simon did.

Cass looked up and down the list she'd created in her head and realized she was going to have to make a decision about what she was willing to do to get past the two men guarding her. They were the first part of the process of gaining her freedom. If there were only one of them, perhaps Cass could have lured him away from his post somehow. There was no way that would work with both men, though.

If only she had a way to re-access the Mantle. She'd tried several times a day to find an access point outside of the firewall but had no luck. Her parents hadn't told Mr. Benson about her directly, but they did get him to shut further access points through the firewall which pretty much removed any chance of her making a connection outside of the enclave.

It was a shame she couldn't download anything from the AI system to help her escape. She'd heard once that some implants could learn muscle memory sequences that enabled the user to do certain extraordinary things. It sounded more like something out of a holovid than real life, but it would've been helpful.

Cass snorted a derisive laugh at herself. She'd sunk pretty far if she'd started thinking she was going to be able to get some sort of superpowers from the Mantle like they did on the shows she liked to watch at school. If she wanted to get away, Cass was going to have to do it on her own, using only the things she had available to her right now.

Cass monitored the guards' activities as best she could once Simon left. Two shifts came to the house over the course of a 24-hour span. She realized that at some point, the guards took a break in the middle of the night. One of them always went to get coffee or some food from the kitchen while the other one remained in position. If she waited until that moment, she'd only have to deal with one of them at a time. It still didn't give her much of a chance fighting her way past even one fully-grown adult male but it was better than taking on two of them.

Cass lay down in bed and stared at the ceiling as she began to put the pieces of her plan together in her head. As she did, she was fully aware of how easy it would be for any step along the way to end in total failure. There was only going to be one chance to get this right, slim as it was. She had to be ready to take it.

Cass had all day to work on refining her plans. Nothing could be done until the middle of the night when everyone else but the guards were asleep. She decided to check over the plans a few more times, then try to get some extra sleep. She'd need it since it was likely she'd be up all night trying to get away if her plan worked.

Chapter 24

IT WAS NEARLY two in the morning when her internal auditory implant alerted her to the sound of one of the guards leaving the area by the front door. She heard him walking through the house over the hardwood floors to the kitchen. His boots made a distinctive clumping sound on the wood. Cass had set her auditory system and implant to listen for movement downstairs by the guards after the house had settled down.

Cass sat up. It was time to put her cobbled-together plan into action.

She rolled out of bed fully dressed. Even her shoes were on. It was just a question of when to make her move. Cass went over to her desk and picked up one of her soccer trophies. The trophy was pretty heavy and the base was made of simulated marble. She figured if she held it by the figurine at the top, she could swing it like a club. It was also small enough that she could conceal it behind her as she went down the stairs. It wasn't much, but it was all she had.

Cass left her room and tiptoed down the hallway until she reached the top of the stairs. Peeking around the corner, Cass saw the single guard standing by the door. He was checking something on his phone and he leaned up against the front door with his back to the bottom of the stairs. The other one clattered around in the kitchen. It sounded like he was getting something out of the refrigerator.

Cass decided to walk quickly and confidently down the stairs as if she was planning on going somewhere in the house as part of her regular routine. She kept her left hand at her side to conceal the makeshift trophy-club. Her right hand slid down the banister, tapping her fingers as she went down the steps to try and draw the man's attention away from her other arm.

Because he was turned partially away from her, he didn't spot her until she was halfway down the stairs. Her presence startled him as he looked up from checking messages on his phone.

"Miss, you need to go back to your room. We have orders and you're not to be up roaming the house at night."

Cass kept moving as she answered. She was almost to the bottom. "I'm hungry and I need to get something to eat. My blood sugar is too low. I didn't finish my dinner."

"That's not my problem, miss. I'm serious, you need to go back upstairs, now."

The man started forward as Cass reached the bottom step. He pointed up the steps and shook his head, still trying to tell her to turn around. With the ferocity of a week of imprisonment and humiliation behind it, she swung her left arm up as hard as she could, aiming the base of the trophy at the side of the guard's head.

Cass didn't know who was more surprised by the success of her attack, the guard or her. His brief shocked expression changed over to a blank stare as his eyes rolled back in his head and he slumped to the floor.

She stepped over the body at the bottom of the steps. Cass hoped he was just unconscious and not dead. She couldn't stand having another death on her hands. She stopped for a brief moment and leaned down over the collapsed man. A wave of relief washed over her as she realized he was still breathing.

Cass clutched the trophy tighter in her left hand and started towards the kitchen. One down, one to go. As Cass made her way down the hallway towards the kitchen, she couldn't figure out what the guard in there was doing. She realized, as she got closer, that he was eating something else while he was preparing whatever other food he'd found in the fridge. He had not heard anything of her scuffle with his companion. That gave her a fighting chance when she got to the kitchen.

Cass held the trophy at her left side again, ready to strike. She angled her body a little bit to keep the makeshift club hidden as she walked into the kitchen from the hallway. The second guard stood at the island counter in the center of the room, making two sandwiches using lunch meat and cheese from the fridge, along with some club rolls he must have found in the cabinet by the toaster.

"Hey, Charlie, do you want mustard on this..." The guard looked up and stopped as he realized it wasn't his partner coming into the kitchen. "Hey, kid, what are you doing down here. Why didn't Charlie put you back up in your room?"

"I think Charlie went to the bathroom or something. He wasn't there when I came downstairs just now."

"Hey, Charlie," the guard called past Cass for his partner. "Are you out there?"

His eyes narrowed when he got no answer. Cass wasn't nearly close enough to make this work, but she had to try. He was already getting suspicious. Cass charged at the guard, running around the side of the island countertop, bringing her arm up in a wild, roundhouse swing at his head the way she had against the first guard.

Unfortunately, this guy was prepared for her attack. His suspicious nature paid off for him and he quickly reached out with one arm to block the incoming blow. He used some sort of fancy maneuver with his free hand and before Cass knew what happened, he'd disarmed her. He threw the trophy to the floor behind him while holding her wrist in an iron grip with one hand. His fingers squeezed hard, grinding the bones in her wrist together.

"Ouch, you're hurting me."

"What do I care. You're not even human anymore so how do I even know you feel pain? You're just a damned sub. What did you do to Charlie?"

"Charlie's taking a little nap, that's all. Maybe he'll wake up and then again maybe he won't."

Her snarky answer earned her another painful squeeze on her wrist. The strength in his grip felt like he could snap the bones in Cass's arm just by twisting his hand.

"Stop it, that's enough. I won't try to get away, I promise." Cass hissed her words through gritted teeth as she tried not to cry out. There was still a chance she could get away, but only if she kept from waking up the rest of the family. Somehow, Cass had to break away from this guy and make a run for it.

"I see you eyeballing the door girlie-girl. You can't get away because we have all the doors locked and monitored. Right now, you're going to come over here and sit down while I handcuff you to this chair."

He hauled Cass over to one of the kitchen barstools. The guard sat her down on one of them and brought her hands down to her side. A few seconds later, he clapped something cold and metal around her wrist and she felt it click shut and ratchet closed till it was tight against her skin. He slipped the other end of the handcuff through the rungs in the back of the chair, then attached it to her other wrist so that she was bound not just with her arms behind her back, but also secured to the chair itself.

"Ouch, you're hurting me again."

"Shut up. I have to go check on Charlie. You stay here."

Cass didn't have a choice. The bar stools were made of cast-iron and were very heavy. Even if she could manage to pick up the stool she was cuffed to, she wouldn't get very far out of the house with it before she was caught. Cass tugged and pulled at the painful tightness of the handcuffs, but it was no use. Her plan had failed. It was over.

Chapter 25

A SMALL NOISE behind Cass drew her attention. Her mother came into the room from the doorway leading to the driveway.

"Cassie, what are you doing up?"

Cass's anger made her lose all pretense of being up for innocent reasons. "What do you think I'm doing, Mother. I'm trying to get away before you all kill me tomorrow."

Her mom came over to Cass and bent down on the other side of the island, picking up the trophy.

Cass's mom shook her head. She glanced up as the guard reentered the kitchen.

"Oh, hello ma'am. I'm glad you're up. Your daughter here injured my partner and I have to call in to have back up come and replace him. We have orders to maintain two people here at all times."

"Not a problem at all. I'm sorry she did that. Apparently, she used this." Cass's mom held up the trophy as the other guard nodded.

"Yes, she tried to hit me with it, too. If you hold onto it for a little bit, I probably should get it as evidence. Mr. Cantwell will want to know what she did."

Her mom smiled and nodded. "No problem at all. Go ahead and make your call. I'll go and put it in the other room by the door. That way, you won't forget it."

The guard nodded thanks and started tapping something on his phone before holding it up to his ear to make the call.

What happened next caught Cass completely by surprise. As soon as the guard turned away from her mother, she raised the trophy overhead and brought it crashing down on the back of the man's neck. He fell to his knees, knocked down but definitely not knocked out. The guard twisted around to try and grab the weapon from her.

Her mom dodged his initial attempts to grab the trophy and swung two more times, hitting him in the back of the head and on the shoulder. She kept swinging repeatedly as the man crumpled on the far side of the island from where Cass sat. After the guy disappeared, the only thing Cass could see was her mother swinging the trophy again and again and again.

Her mother finally stopped and set the trophy down on the countertop, now covered in splatters of blood. Some of the splatters covered her face, too.

Her mother's satisfied smile beaming amidst the blood dripping down her cheeks was an image Cass wouldn't soon forget. "I don't think he'll be bothering us anymore. I'd slipped sleeping pills into their midnight snacks, but this'll work, too."

Cass's mom gave her daughter another half-smile and bent down again, disappearing behind the counter. She puttered around out of sight for a few seconds, then stood up, holding the guard's keys in her hand.

Moving behind Cass, it took her mom a few tries, but she eventually found the one that opened the handcuffs. Cass pulled her arms back in front of her and massaged her sore wrists.

"Come on, Cass. We have to hurry. There's a narrow window of time before the next set of guards gets here to take over and by then, I need to be back in the house in bed."

Cass stared at her mother, trying to understand what was happening.

"Cass, get up and follow me. Don't freeze up now. We can't stay here, sweetie. We have to get you out."

"Out?"

"Yes, out. Now, come on. We don't have much time."

Her mom reached out and grabbed at Cass's hand, dragging her towards the kitchen door. Cass shuffled along behind her mother, still unsure of what was going on. Her mother hadn't said more than five words to her at a time since discovering the truth about her implants. Now, her mom led Cass outside as if she was trying to help her escape. It didn't make any sense.

Her mom pushed Cass into the front passenger seat of the car before moving around to the driver's side. "We have to hurry before anyone finds out you're gone."

As her mother climbed in behind the wheel and started the car, Cass asked, "Mom, what are you doing?"

"I'm getting you away from here. I can't let them hurt you anymore. I hate that you have that thing in your head, but I'm not going to let them kill you, or worse, leave you only half alive. At least this way, I know you'll have a fighting chance and maybe even manage to get away."

Cass sat in the front seat staring straight ahead, her mind swimming through a sea of emotions as her mother backed the car out of the driveway. Until this moment, she was sure her mother had disowned her and stopped caring about her at all.

They drove through the darkened streets of the enclave, until they reached an area of the walled enclosure on the opposite side of the compound from their home. It was near the doctor's office and the enclave market. It was nowhere near the entrance to the community.

"Mom, what's over here? Shouldn't we go out the main gate?"

"No, too many cameras there. I also wouldn't put it past Simon Cantwell to have someone watching the front gate at night for an escape. Plus, his guards moved from the motel in town to stay on cots in the Rec Center. They're too close to the entrance for comfort if we get stopped for any reason."

Her mom pulled the car up behind some buildings near the tall, concrete enclosure wall. It was topped with coils of barbed wire.

Her mom got out and motioned for Cass to follow her. "There's a hole in the camera system over here that hasn't been repaired for some time. The enclave doesn't have the funds it used to have and a lot of the security cameras, while due for replacement, haven't been upgraded."

"How do you know all this?"

"Cadence's mom, Maisy. She knows everything her husband does with security around here. She happened to let it slip a while ago that the cameras at this end of the enclave weren't working. She joked about how easy it would be for someone to sneak in and rob the stores and offices here."

Her mom pointed up to the wall above them. "Anyone going over the wall here won't be seen at all, especially if they cover their tracks."

"What about my implant and the firewall?"

"It's all supported by the camera system. The cameras are down, so the wireless signal repeaters for the firewall are down as well." Her mom smiled in the darkness. "Maisy really talks too much."

Cass looked up. The wall around the enclave was at least eight feet tall here and that didn't count the barbed wire. Cass wasn't sure how she was going to get over it.

"Mom, do you have a ladder or something?"

"No, but the others do."

Her mom pulled her phone from her pocket and tapped a message onto it then stood waiting for an answer. A few seconds later, there was the ping of an incoming message on her mom's phone accompanied by a noise from the far side of the wall. Something scraped along the opposite side of the concrete from where they stood.

The scraping continued until a minute later, a figure wearing all black appeared in the darkness atop the wall climbing up from the outside. The newcomer reached out to the sharpened wire coils and tugged at them. They had a tool of some sort in their hand. Cass was so stunned at the speed with which all of this was happening, she didn't even think to dial in her ocular implant to see better in the darkness.

The person on the other side of the wall worked for several more seconds until they managed to cut an opening in the wire. They slid the coils back in both directions far enough to leave a gap big enough for a person to climb through.

Her mom moved forward towards the base of the wall. "Come on, Cassie. We have to hurry before we're spotted. I'll help you climb up."

Her mother bent down to form a stirrup with her interlaced fingers. Cass placed her foot in it and put her hands flat against the wall to steady herself as she prepared to step up and reach for the top.

The shadowy figure above her had their sweatshirt hood pulled up. It obscured their face at first. It wasn't until the familiar metal hand extended down from the top of the wall to help pull her up that Cass realized who it was.

"Shelby? Is it really you?"

"In the flesh, roomy. Come on. Grab my wrist. Your mom's right. We don't have much time."

Cass turned to her mother. "You called her? But how?"

"I have my ways. I used to be pretty good at cybersecurity myself before I met your father. Once we got together and you girls were born, I stopped working. I've tried to keep my skills up over the years, even though I don't work anymore. It was hard to track her down, but I managed it."

Shelby had pushed her hood back and Cass could see her face now. She smiled down at her girlfriend. "Smart women think alike, Cass. Your mom helped us avoid the Sapiens First hit squad that was sent after us and brought us here to get you."

Her mom smiled and gestured at Shelby on the wall above them. "I never thought I would use my old skills for something like this, but I'm glad I stayed current on things."

Cass reached out and pulled her mother close in a tight embrace. Her mother returned the hug, stroking her hand down the back of Cass's head like she used to when Cass was little.

After a few seconds, she released her daughter. "Come on, I'll give you a boost and Shelby can pull you up the rest of the way. I have to get the car back to the house before they know you're gone. The longer we can keep them guessing, the better."

She bent over, cupping her hands together again so that Cass could get a boost up to the top of the wall.

Cass stepped into her mother's hands and pushed up with her leg while her mom lifted. Cass reached out for Shelby's extended hand coming down from the top. She grasped the familiar warm metal appendage and held on.

Her mother lifted higher from below while Shelby pulled from the top. Soon Cass scrambled through the narrow gap in the wire until she'd straddled the top of the wall. A stepladder sat propped against the outside of the wall next to a small, white minivan.

Shelby leaned forward from where she sat atop the wall and hugged Cass.

"I can't believe it's really you, Shel. It's like a dream." Cass paused and squeezed Shelby tight. "I'm sorry about your parents."

Shelby released the embrace and nodded to Cass as she leaned back. "We can talk later. Right now, swing your leg over and climb down the ladder. Someone might come along the roads on either side at any time even though it's late."

A voice from inside the van called up to them. "Hurry up ladies, we don't have all day." Cass saw a woman get out of the driver's side. She stood even taller than Shelby, with short spiky red hair jutting up from the top of her head. The newcomer pointed to the bottom of the ladder. "Come on."

Cass spared one glance back at her mother looking up at her from the other side, waved once, then she slid down until her feet reached the top of the ladder. It was just a few feet below the wall. She turned to face the stepladder and climbed down the rest of the way.

By the time she reached the bottom, Shelby had rearranged the coils of barbed wire above them to hide their escape route and climbed down the ladder to join her at the bottom. Together, she and Cass collapsed the ladder and shoved it into van's open rear doors.

As soon as they shut the two doors, Cass pulled Shelby into another embrace, holding her close.

"I was so afraid they'd found you, Shel. I'm sorry. I didn't mean to tell them where you were."

"That's all right, Cass. My cousin, Ramona, was one step ahead of them the whole time. Once we got the warning from your mother, we knew they were coming. We'd already moved on to a safe location by the time they arrived at her old place. Then your mother told me how she planned on getting you out. I rushed down here to help her so you could get away."

Cass glanced back at the wall as she climbed in the back seat of the van. She wanted to ask her mother so many questions. She knew she'd probably never get that chance now. Shelby got in the back next to her and shut the sliding van door.

Ramona tapped a command on the dashboard's control screen and the van pulled away from the grassy shoulder onto the road. She looked back over her shoulder at the two women in the seat behind her.

"It's time to make you disappear, Cass. Are you ready to go on the run?"

Cass shrugged. She didn't know what she wanted, other than to be sitting here next to Shelby.

Ramona laughed and turned around, lifting her foot up to rest on the dash as the automated van drove away.

Ten minutes later, they pulled onto a highway, headed west, putting miles and miles between them and the enclave.

Cass rested her head on Shelby's shoulder. All she'd wanted for so long had been to hold on to her girlfriend's hand again. Now, the two of them were on the run together, searching for the cyber underground.

Like the story? Leave a review.

Cass Armstrong's story continues with
Cyber's Underground - Book 3
coming soon.

Afterword

A Note From The Author

It's always interesting how things happening in the world around me seem to reflect what I'm writing at any given time. I think this happens because as I ponder the challenges and conflicts faced by my books' characters, I become more aware of people facing those same challenges in the world outside my home.

As I wrote Cyber's Escape and dealt with Cass's parents, the Sapiens Movement, and their attempt to exert control over Cass's person and beliefs, I was struck by several news stories about daughters fleeing repression from their families and countries. There were also countries in the news proposing new laws making being a homosexual a death penalty offense. The cliche that life is stranger than fiction may better be written as fiction reflects life in all its cruel strangeness and rich diversity.

In much of the world, women and girls are in positions where control over their bodies and individuality are in the hands of repressive, patriarchal families and governments. Stories persist about young women fleeing these repressive situations where they're stopped as they try to complete their refugee journeys just short of their final destinations. Their families and home governments exert diplomatic control to interrupt travel and cancel visas while they're en route to a final destination in a country ready to receive them with open arms.

In light of this, Cass's struggle to escape the plans her father and the Sapiens Movement leadership have for her isn't so far-fetched. While this story takes place years in the future, in a dystopian America we may not recognize, the possibilities represented in Cass's plight could happen here. Indeed, it is legal today in much of the United States to reject applicants for employment or housing for something as simple as their choice of a partner in life. People I love and care about have faced such discrimination.

The story gets pretty dark in places as I explore these themes, especially when Simon tortures Cass to get Shelby's location. It was important to show how dehumanizing a person, for whatever reason, makes it easier to do unspeakable things to them and pass it off as reasonable in our minds.

I was asked by a beta reader who got an early look at the story how James and Faye Armstrong could stand idly by and let a man torture their daughter in their home. We know Faye ultimately didn't stand for it, and eventually helped Cass escape.

James, however, justified it in two ways. She had the chance to answer questions willingly and turned it down. That made it her fault in his eyes. He also knew, according to his beliefs, it wasn't really his daughter in that body anymore. She'd only return once the hardware was removed.

Standing up for people and their right to self-determination and self-actualization is the responsibility of each of us. Dystopian futures represent potential futures that could come to pass if we're not careful.

I try to remember this as I go about my life. My everyday choices, words, and social media posts have real consequences with ripple effects I cannot fully appreciate, especially if my eyes and mind are closed to the repercussions.

Afterword

I hope you all enjoy the next chapter in this story as the trilogy concludes with Cyber's Underground. Don't hesitate to reach out to me with your questions and comments. In the meantime, be at peace and share some kindness today.

Also by Jamie Davis

Get a free book. Visit JamieDavisBooks.com

Sapiens Run Trilogy

Book 1 - *Cyber's Change*

Book 2 - *Cyber's Escape*

Book 3 - *Cyber's Underground*

—

The Delivery Mage (5 books)

Book 1 - *Deliver or Die*

—

The Broken Throne Series (5 books)

Read book 1 - *The Charm Runner*

—

The Accidental Traveler LitRPG Trilogy

(with C.J. Davis)

Read book 1 - *The Accidental Thief*

—

Accidental Champion Trilogy

(with C.J. Davis)

Read book 1 - *Accidental Duelist*

—

Extreme Medical Services Series (8 books)

Read book 1 - Extreme Medical Services

—

About the Author

Jamie Davis is a nurse, retired paramedic, author, and nationally recognized medical educator who began teaching new emergency responders as a training officer for his local EMS program. He loves everything fantasy and sci-fi and especially the places where stories intersect with his love of medicine or gaming.

Jamie lives in a home in the woods in Maryland with his wife, three children, and dog.

He loves hearing from readers and going to cons and events where he meets up with fans. Reach out and say "hi." Visit Jamie-DavisBooks.com for more books, free offers and more!

Follow Jamie Online
www.jamiedavisbooks.com